"He wanted a son, and he got me!"

Heather turned away from Daniel to hide the pain now clouding her eyes. She had told her fiancé only a half truth, the wound from her late stepfather's rejection—although but a memory—was still raw.

"And he wanted money, but instead he got *me*!" Daniel countered in his harsh rasp. "He knew I never wanted you as a wife—but now it seems we have each other!"

Heather wanted to believe that Daniel was capable of love—but he didn't seem to care for anyone. Even now, loving him as she did, Heather wished—ironically—there was something she could do to release Daniel from this tie to her he obviously didn't want. But there was nothing she *could* do.

CAROLE MORTIMER, one of our most popular—and prolific—English authors, began writing in the Harlequin Presents series in 1979. She now has more than forty top-selling romances to her credit and shows no signs whatever of running out of plot ideas. She writes strong traditional romances with a distinctly modern appeal, and her winning way with characters and romantic plot twists has earned her an enthusiastic audience worldwide.

Books by Carole Mortimer

Don't miss any of our special offers. Write to us at the following address for information on our newest releases.

Harlequin Reader Service
901 Fuhrmann Blvd., P.O. Box 1397, Buffalo, NY 14240
Canadian address: P.O. Box 603,
Fort Erie, Ont. L2A 5X3

CAROLE MORTIMER

taggart's woman

Harlequin Books

TORONTO • NEW YORK • LONDON
AMSTERDAM • PARIS • SYDNEY • HAMBURG
STOCKHOLM • ATHENS • TOKYO • MILAN

Mum and Dad,
Wishing you many more happy
years together,
We love you.

Harlequin Presents first edition February 1988
ISBN 0-373-11050-2

Original hardcover edition published in 1987
by Mills & Boon Limited

CHAPTER ONE

As PARTIES went, this was a good one. But then, all the parties at the Danvers' house were sure to be good, the social successes of the year more than one guest had been heard to praise during the evening.

Heather kept a watchful eye on the enjoyment of all her guests, while dividing her time between the groups gathered around talking, making sure that no one was left out, that everyone was either dancing, talking, eating, or flirting, as she was. No one came to a Danvers' party and claimed to be bored. Except, perhaps, for one man.

Her violet gaze flickered to him in annoyance. He was standing slightly apart from everyone else, looking as though he had dressed for a party in the black evening suit and snowy white shirt, even holding a partially drunk glass of champagne in his hand. And yet Heather didn't need to be any closer to him than the length of the room to know he was looking down his contemptuous nose at both her and her guests!

Her father had always insisted on inviting his business partner to every social function they held, not because he liked the other man, but because he enjoyed seeing how uncomfortable

Daniel Taggart was among people who merely tolerated him because of his wealth, rather than liked the man himself. Heather had invited Daniel for quite a different reason.

Why couldn't he at least try to *look* as if he were enjoying himself—even if he wasn't? She was no happier with this situation than he was, but at least everyone *thought* she was!

She stopped to chat with several people on her way over to Daniel's side, seeming as if she were ecstatically happy, all the time getting closer and closer to him, watching as he threw the remains of his champagne to the back of his throat before reaching for another glass from one of the circulating waiters. In the two years Heather had known him she had never seen Daniel drunk, but there was a first time for everything!

At last she reached his side, the warm smile curving her lips not reaching the coldness of her eyes. 'Could you stop swilling vintage champagne back as if it were water?' she hissed vehemently.

'Or beer, *Miss Danvers*?' he taunted, taking another large swallow of the bubbly wine.

Her cheeks became flushed, her eyes flashing warningly. 'The only snob standing here, *Mr Taggart,* is *you*,' she snapped.

'Oh, really?' Grey eyes were narrowed angrily. 'Then maybe I should leave——'

'Don't you dare!' she warned furiously. 'It may have escaped your notice, but you are supposed to be co-host of this party.'

'This isn't a *party*,' he scorned, slamming his glass down angrily on the table. 'It's one last parting joke from Max to me!'

'And me,' she rasped bitterly.

Daniel's gaze raked over her scathingly. 'Heather Danvers, the socialite daughter of Max Danvers, marrying the self-made millionaire Daniel Taggart, for whom the rough edges haven't even begun to be smoothed—how will you stand it, my dear!' he derided with contempt.

The colour came and then went again in her cheeks, her eyes hugely purple. She knew the figure she presented tonight, the black gown clinging alluringly to her slender curves, her bare arms and shoulders deeply tanned, her hair a swathe of midnight-black waves falling to just below her shoulders, her make-up perfect; everything about her was as elegantly beautiful as the daughter of Maximilian Danvers should be.

She had dressed this way for the party that celebrated her engagement and forthcoming marriage to the man at her side who looked at her so disdainfully!

One last parting joke from her father, Daniel had said. Only there was nothing in the least funny about the two of them being forced to marry to maintain complete control over the airline her father had built up over the last twenty years, and in which Daniel Taggart had become a partner two years ago.

The illness that had been eating away at her father's body for a year before his death six months ago had embittered him more than any of them had realised, the reading of his will revealing that Heather could only inherit her share of the company if she married Daniel Taggart, and that, should they fail to marry within one year after his death, his shares were to be sold on the open market to the highest bidder, except, he stipulated, to Daniel Taggart himself. He had also neatly taken care of Heather choosing the money over marriage to Daniel Taggart, by stating that any money made by the sale of the shares was to be given to numerous charities.

Heather felt as though he had physically slapped her from the grave as she sat in on the will-reading, knowing why he punished her, denying her the one thing he knew she wanted. Her father had hated her and had never lost an opportunity, within the privacy of their home, to let her know how he felt about her. Even in death he wasn't going to let her forget that.

He had hated Daniel Taggart too, for coming along with the money he needed when the airline began to falter, had reluctantly made the other man his partner rather than lose his company completely. Now he was forcing Daniel to accept Heather as his wife or risk losing the control over the company that now meant so much to him. Daniel knew that if it came to selling the shares he could lose everything he had worked for since he had made the company a profitable one again. Her father had even hated him for that. Daniel Taggart was a man who had clawed his way up from his poor beginning to the point where he had the millions her father needed to keep his company running, and, according to Max—although Heather was inclined to mistrust the opinion because of his bitterness!—Daniel hadn't always done it honestly.

Her father had treated the other man with grudging respect, never losing an opportunity to belittle him or make things uncomfortable for him. A final joke, Daniel called this last vindictiveness, only her father's idea of a joke was to hurt someone, and this time he had hit out at the two people he most seemed to despise.

She had been nineteen when she had first met Daniel, and had found him attractive in an austere sort of way. But he had lost no time in letting her know that, at thirteen years his junior, he considered her too immature to even notice. Now, two years later, he was being forced to notice her, to take her as his wife. And his contempt was obvious.

'I'll cope,' she rasped. 'Will you?'

Grey eyes raked over her critically, and Heather's breath caught in her throat at the beauty of those eyes; gun-metal grey ringed by black. Daniel was a man who possessed presence rather than surface handsomeness, his face harshly powerful, thick hair as black as her own styled to his ears and collar, dark brows jutting out over those beautiful eyes, his nose long and straight, his mouth a sculptured slash above a strongly square jaw. Tall and powerful, he had all the rugged grace of an athlete. And, as he claimed so derisively, none of the rough edges of his childhood had been smoothed, neither by his wealth nor his success.

He and her father had been as different as any two men could be, her father a product of the charmingly false society he had lived in all his life, Daniel bluntly honest to the point of rudeness. Of the two she preferred the latter, having been on the receiving end of her father's charmingly laced barbs too often not to appreciate open hostility when she encountered it.

'With you as my wife?' Daniel derided scornfully. 'No doubt I'll survive.'

Her gaze didn't falter as she met his challenge. Survive, would he? She wasn't sure *she* would! For years she had been searching for the man whom she could love and one day proudly call husband, and now it seemed she was to have this cold stranger as that very important person in her life. She wasn't naïve, she knew that not all marriages took place because the couple were in love; she had just never imagined hers would be a marriage of convenience.

'Will you?' she taunted. 'Then maybe you could start acting a little as if it isn't a prison sentence!'

'Oh, I realise that,' he bit out. 'I can't get any time off for good behaviour!'

He might not think his barbs hurt her, the cool sophisticate, but they did! 'I doubt that you'll be good,' she retorted hardily. 'I doubt either of us will,' she hissed with scorn.

His eyes narrowed. 'If you think that I'm going to meekly stand by while you flaunt an affair with Wingate, or someone like him——'

'I have no intention of having an affair with Phillip or any other man once we're married,' she snapped, her year-long friendship with Phillip over from the moment she had agreed to become Daniel's wife. She had no doubt that, once she was married to him, Daniel would be quite enough for any woman to cope with in her life! 'Can you say the same?'

His mouth twisted. 'Don't you think these little problems should have been sorted out *before* you agreed to marry me and threw this party to tell all your friends? After all, I'm due to make the announcement soon.'

'Your neat avoidance of an answer tells me that you have every intention of continuing to see—Sandra, isn't her name?' she said, coldly dismissive.

His expression darkened. 'I didn't avoid giving you an answer. And her name is Cassandra,' he corrected drily, seeming to know that Heather had been fully aware of his mistress's name. 'Are you going to be a wife to me?'

Heather swallowed hard at the bluntness of the question. 'We're to be married in a month——'

'I'm not talking about wearing my ring and calling yourself Mrs Taggart,' he drawled. 'I'm talking about being my woman, sharing my bed, giving that delectable body to me——'

'As you said, I think we should have discussed

this at some other time.' She was rigid with embarrassment.

'Too crude for you?' Daniel arched dark brows. 'Perhaps I should have asked if we're going to *fully* cohabit?'

Sleep with this man, make love with him? It sounded a little like hell—and heaven! 'Maybe we shouldn't make the announcement until we're both a little more sure of what we want from this relationship——'

'Don't be a fool, Heather,' his voice was harsh. 'We want to keep control of Air International, *that's* what we want from this relationship!'

'And—er—the other?' She moistened the dryness of her lips.

He shrugged broad shoulders. 'We can sort that out some other time.' He glanced at his watch, his hands long and powerful. 'The witching-hour is upon us,' he drawled drily.

He hated the thought of this marriage, and she couldn't blame him, hating it herself; but what choice did either of them have?

She stood back and watched him as he moved away from this position for the first time during the evening, silencing the small band that played at the other end of the room, taking over the microphone as all the guests gave him their full attention.

Her palms felt damp, her legs shaky, a sense of panic making her want to run, and keep on running. And then Daniel began to speak, and a sudden feeling of calm assailed her, completely in control again.

'Ladies and gentlemen,' his voice was warm and smooth, infused with a friendliness Heather knew he was far from feeling towards the people who had mainly been friends of her father's, 'my fiancée, Heather Danvers.' He held out his hand for her to join him as everyone began to clap, almost everybody in the room having already known of the reason for the party. And those that didn't hid their surprise behind a polite show of enthusiasm.

Heather didn't doubt she and Daniel would provide after-dinner conversation for weeks to come. The full contents of her father's will had been kept within the privacy of the family circle and most of the people here assumed this to be a love-match. Unlikely as that might seem between the two of them, Heather preferred that to everyone thinking they were marrying for purely mercenary reasons!

She reached Daniel's side in a flurry of congratulations, her hand taken firmly in his as family and friends gathered around to ply them both with questions. When was the wedding? Where were they going on their honeymoon? Where were they going to live after the wedding?

She glanced at Daniel at the last. It was another one of those questions they had never got around to asking each other. There had been so much else to do over the last six months, and then this party to arrange when they decided the only thing they *could* do was marry, that

the details just hadn't been worked out. She
realised now that perhaps they should have
been.

Where *would* they live once they were married?
This house had been left as another part of her
inheritance, had been her home all her life, but
Daniel never seemed to be comfortable when he
was here, and she couldn't see him wanting to
set up home here for any reason. If the truth
were known, she would rather sell the place,
too, and make a fresh start away from all the
memories.

'Details, details,' her uncle Lionel dismissed
laughingly. 'I propose we drink a toast to the
happy couple.'

Heather gave him a grateful smile. Her father's
younger brother, he had never shown her
anything but kindness, and she didn't know
what she would have done without him during
the last six months. He had been her father's
assistant from the time Max first began the
airline, had been happy to continue helping
Daniel in the same way, and had also helped
Heather with all the arrangements after her
father's death. In fact, over the years, she had
felt closer to Uncle Lionel than to the man she
called Father!

'Heather and Daniel!' He beamed at them
both once everyone had a glass of champagne
in their hand.

Heather smiled awkwardly as the toast was
drunk in their honour, pointedly keeping her
face averted from the brief glimpse she had had

of Daniel's sardonic expression. But she had to agree with the thought she knew was going through his mind; anyone who could believe the two of them were marrying because they loved each other was either blind or a complete romantic. And she doubted many of the people here tonight were the latter, although their complete self-interest often made them the former!

She received a jolt as she looked sceptically at their guests and found Phillip glowering at the two of them. He looked as if he hated her at that moment!

She couldn't exactly blame him for being angry with her, they had been seeing each other on a regular basis for almost a year, and then a month ago she had had to tell him of her decision to marry Daniel. One of Air International's youngest executives, Phillip hadn't taken the news well, had accused her of marrying the man with the most money. Perhaps in the circumstances his bitterness had been understandable, but she had genuinely liked him, wouldn't have continued to see him exclusively for that length of time if she hadn't, and it had hurt her to give up his friendship.

Several other guests were looking at him speculatively too, and, with a mocking inclination of his golden head in her direction, he threw the champagne to the back of his throat before slamming the glass down and walking out.

Her eyes widened as she looked about her

awkwardly to see who else had witnessed his abrupt departure.

Grey eyes met hers mockingly, and Daniel bent his head as if to nuzzle against her throat. 'Maybe you should have told your lover about your father's will,' he mocked. 'He seems a trifle put out!'

She stiffened in his arms, turning slightly as if to kiss the powerful line of his jaw. 'I suppose Cassandra is quite happy to continue to be your mistress even when you have a wife?' she taunted.

He straightened, his mouth taut, his eyes glittering dangerously. 'You——'

'Speech, Daniel,' her uncle demanded cheerfully. Lionel was tall and loose-limbed, with hair almost as black as Heather's, although his was liberally sprinkled with grey in his fifty-fifth year.

'Yes, Daniel,' drawled Stella, Lionel's wife of the last five years, twenty years her husband's junior, beautifully exotic in the clinging red gown that made her hair appear like spun gold. 'Do tell us all how you and Heather fell in love.'

Heather felt her cheeks burn under her aunt's derision. Not that she was allowed to call the other woman Aunt, Stella insisting she was far too young for the title. And Stella knew damn well that she and Daniel hadn't 'fallen in love'; as a member of the family she was well aware of the contents of her father's will.

Daniel looked at the older woman mockingly.

'The same way most couples fall in love,' he said drily.

'But it was *so* sudden,' Stella taunted, her blue eyes maliciously bright.

He gave an inclination of his head. 'As sudden as your own marriage to Lionel five years ago!'

Stella's face flushed at the challenge: before becoming Lionel's wife she had been his secretary for several months. Heather had always thought the other woman's motives slightly mercenary, but Daniel's challenge was as close as anyone had ever come to saying so outright. And Stella obviously didn't like to be reminded of her more humble beginnings, having firmly established herself in this society over the last five years.

She put her arm through the crook of her husband's, smiling up at him brightly. 'Love can be rather sneaky in its unexpectedness, can't it?' she purred.

Heather shot Daniel a relieved smile as she realised he had won that battle. Stella was hardly in a position to 'throw stones'! 'Daniel?' she prompted huskily, their guests still waiting expectantly.

He nodded abruptly, turning back to their guests. 'Heather has kindly consented to be my wife,' he told them evenly. 'The wedding will be next month, and——'

'Next month?' one of the female guests exclaimed incredulously.

Daniel arched questioning brows at the

blushing woman. 'Is there some problem with that?'

'Er—no, of course not.' Heather recognised the woman as a friend of Stella's. 'I just—it isn't long,' she excused lamely.

'No,' he acknowledged drily. 'But you're all welcome to come to another party here in three months' time, and I'm sure you will find Heather as slender then as she is now!'

Heather's uncle gave an uncomfortable cough. 'I'm sure Rita didn't mean——'

'It's all right, Lionel,' Daniel sighed. 'The truth of the matter is, what man in his right mind *would* want to wait any length of time to make Heather his bride?' Several of the male guests gave an appreciative murmur, and Daniel gave them an acknowledging smile of his good luck in being the man to make Heather *his* bride. 'As I was saying,' he began again point-edly, 'Heather and I will be married next month, and I'm sure you—and several hundred others!—will all be invited. For the moment, I suggest we all continue to enjoy the party!'

As if on signal the band began to play a slow love song, and everyone moved back expect-antly, leaving Heather and Daniel at the centre of attention.

She turned to him with frantic eyes. 'They're expecting us to dance!'

'I'm not completely stupid,' he rasped, taking her in his arms to move expertly around the room in time to the music. 'And I do know *how* to dance!'

She knew that, had watched him with other women. Strange, but in all the time she had known him, all the parties he had come to here, she had never danced with him before tonight. For such a big man he moved with a natural grace, in complete command as he guided their movements, his steps smooth and sure.

'I didn't mean——'

'Just dance, Heather,' he snapped. 'And let's get this over with!'

It was 'over with' soon enough, Daniel not speaking to her again as their bodies occasionally touched, releasing her as the music came to an end to ask Stella to dance, leaving her with her uncle. She absently took the glass of wine her uncle handed her, watching the other couple as they moved fluidly together. They were of a similar height, Stella several inches taller than her own five foot five inches, and with the three-inch heels on her sandals Stella's body matched Daniel's perfectly, a fact she seemed to take note of as she danced much too closely to Daniel in Heather's opinion.

On the few occasions Heather had seen them together Daniel hadn't seemed overly fond of Stella, and yet surely the couple were speaking together more warmly, and dancing together more closely, than their relationship required?

She glanced at her uncle, receiving an affectionate smile in return before he turned to watch his wife admiringly. Oh well, if he didn't mind she was sure she shouldn't either. But somehow it didn't seem quite right to see her aunt dancing so intimately with the man *she* intended to marry, even if it wasn't a love-match.

She turned her back on the dancing couple. 'I hope that you will give me away, Uncle Lionel,' she invited warmly.

'Not because I want to,' he agreed reluctantly, 'even though Daniel is a fine young man.' His eyes twinkled blue-grey. 'I'd rather you had moved in with Stella and me and become the daughter we never had. But,' he sighed, 'I'm sure you and Daniel are doing the right thing.'

Given the choice between moving in with her uncle and Stella, or becoming Daniel's wife, she had no doubt she was making the right choice! She and Stella would have been at each other's throats in a day!

'Let's hope so,' she dismissed lightly, absently noting that Daniel was dancing with one of her friends now.

'I think the conditions in Max's will were completely unfair, but——'

'When did he ever behave any other way?' she finished bitterly. 'He never forgave me for not being the boy he'd wanted!'

Her uncle sighed, his smile regretful. 'Max could be an unreasonable man——'

'You know he could be worse than that.' Her eyes were hard with the memories.

Her uncle frowned. 'In his own way he did care for you, Heather.'

'Then why has he arranged to marry me to a man he despised?' she scorned.

'He didn't despise Daniel,' Uncle Lionel

sighed. 'He resented him——'

'Because he came along at the right time with the money he needed!' Her eyes were bright. 'If I could have proved he was insane when he made that will, Uncle Lionel, then I would have done so, I would have publicly contested it.'

'Daniel, too,' he nodded with a sigh. 'But it was impossible.'

Her father had made certain of that, had made sure every loophole was covered at the time he made his outrageous will. For six months, she and Daniel had consulted their lawyers trying to find a way out of it, and in the end they had had to admit defeat, to accept that her father had won. How he must be laughing at them both!

Maximilian Danvers hadn't been a kind or yielding man, hated to be thwarted in any way, and when *she* had been born instead of the son he had wanted he had received the biggest setback of his life.

Heather grew up knowing he resented her gender, that she was a disappointment to him. She had been sent away to school when she was eight, rarely seeing him after that, even when she came home for the holidays. She hadn't been able to understand how her mother could have loved and married such a coldly self-centred man, let alone had a child by him. But as she got older, and her mother told her the truth, she had respected the fact that at the time her mother had believed she was doing the right thing for everyone.

Pregnant, the father of her child already married and not interested in her pregnancy, her mother had been working for Max Danvers' newly established airline at the time and hadn't known who to turn to for help when she realised she was to have a child. The airline had been small then, with the owner playing quite a large part in the running of it, and Joyce had broken down one day and told Max Danvers of her predicament, her complete desolation. After that, he had begun to take her out, to offer her comfort when she felt so frightened of what the future held for her, until finally he had offered her and her child a home *and* his name. It had seemed like a miracle to her mother, believing that Max Danvers had come to love her as she had him, and she had gratefully accepted his proposal, determined to be as good a wife to him as she possibly could.

It was only after the birth of her child that Joyce had realised what had been expected of her; a daughter was not what Max Danvers wanted at all. It had been then that he had told his wife of his sterility, of the son he had wanted to continue his name, to one day inherit the empire he intended building, and that he had only married her because she was already pregnant!

But, unless he divorced Joyce and found another pregnant woman to become his wife, a daughter was what he had got, and in the end he had decided that even that was better than no child at all, everyone believing Joyce had been pregnant with his child when they were married. Only Uncle Lionel and her parents had known the truth, and it had remained that way until Heather's mother told her about her real father.

She had understood Max's resentment towards her then, his disappointment in her, and she had learnt to live with the fact that he practically ignored her existence most of the time, his barbs only becoming painfully obvious after the death of her mother six years ago, and then only in the privacy of their home where people wouldn't learn that he wasn't her father at all.

Maybe if he had been, the pain of what he was doing to her would have been too much to bear, but over the years, she had learnt to armour herself against the hurt he inflicted.

But he had known how she felt about Daniel, had somehow guessed at the love she felt for him, she was sure, and he was giving her the final punishment for not being the son he wanted, making it impossible for Daniel ever to feel anything but contempt or hate for her; contempt because if she agreed to the marriage she was obviously marrying him for the money she would inherit, or hate because if she refused to marry him she forced him to lose control of his airline.

It was a situation she couldn't possibly win, and her father had known that!

CHAPTER TWO

HEATHER had often wished she could return the hate her father seemed to have for her, but she had grown up believing he *was* her father, and it was very difficult for a child to hate its parents, no matter how cruel they were. Even when her mother had told her the truth she had pitied him rather than hated him, had tried, despite his indifference, to be the sort of daughter he could be proud of. After her mother died she had known he needed her more than ever, although his bitterness was deeper than ever, too.

She had liked Daniel from the day her father first brought him home to dinner, but as it soon become apparent that her father disliked the younger man, she knew that if her father ever learnt of her feelings for his business partner it would be yet another black mark against her and, as Daniel was totally uninterested in her, it had never been necessary. But the day her father's will—she could never think of him in any other way!—was read, she had realised she couldn't have kept her secret hidden very well, for he had made sure she never had the one thing she had always wanted—Daniel's love.

She and Daniel were trapped now, forced to

marry each other. She would have gladly given up the inheritance she felt she had no entitlement to anyway, if it wouldn't have hurt Daniel for her to do so. But she doubted, knowing his opinion of her privileged background, that he would ever believe her motives could be that unmercenary. To convince him she would have to tell him of her love, and pity was the one emotion she refused to accept from him.

'Well, it's all settled now,' she answered her uncle with a bright smile.

'I always thought you and Phillip——'

'I wasn't in love with him, if that's what you mean,' she interrupted with a feeling of betrayal towards the other man. It was true that she had made it clear to Phillip that she didn't care for him in that way, but that hadn't stopped him professing to care for her.

She would have liked to have spared Phillip the painful humiliation she knew he must be feeling at having to witness her engagement to Daniel, but as all the airline's executives had been invited, it would have looked worse to have singled him out in that way.

'I'm glad about that at least,' her uncle squeezed her arm.

'Which isn't to say,' she drawled drily, 'that you aren't going to have a very angry young man working at Air International for a while!'

Her uncle grimaced. 'Maybe I'll give some thought to sending him up to the Manchester office for a while.'

'Sending *who* up to Manchester?' Stella joined

them, light brows arched mockingly. 'Surely you
aren't trying to get rid of Daniel already,
Heather?' she taunted maliciously.

Heather shook her head, steadily meeting the
other woman's gaze. 'We have all the wedding
arrangements to sort out yet. Besides, Daniel
owns the airline, I doubt he could be *sent*
anywhere!'

Stella shrugged. 'Then who is being sent into
exile?' she drawled.

'We were just discussing poor Phillip, my
dear,' her husband put in with a sigh.

'He left, you know,' the other woman snapped
at Heather. 'I think you used him shame-
fully——'

'Stella——'

'She's been leading him around by the nose
for almost a year now, Lionel,' his wife reminded
him waspishly. 'And now, just because that
savage——'

'Stella, that will be enough!' her husband said
with quiet authority. 'Heather is doing the only
thing she can in the circumstances.'

'I always did think Max was slightly vindic-
tive where she was concerned,' Stella scorned,
completely unperturbed by her husband's disapproving frown. 'It's the only reason I can think
of for wishing a man like that on his only
daughter!'

The first part was true and undeniable, but 'a
man like that' rankled; Stella had no reason to
malign Daniel in that way. 'He's a good
man——'

'He's uncouth!' the other woman dismissed disparagingly. 'That remark he made about your not being being pregnant, for instance——'

'And wasn't that what Rita was thinking?' Heather's eyes were deep purple. 'Wasn't that what almost all the people here had assumed?' she scorned.

'I think you're being a little unfair to some of them,' her uncle chided.

'Well, I don't,' she snapped. 'And all because we've decided to marry soon!'

'With undue haste,' Stella corrected pointedly. 'I can't see what all the rush is about personally, you have another six months before Max's deadline is up.'

'Daniel and I discussed waiting,' Heather bit out tautly. 'And we decided that for the good of the airline——' She broke off as Stella gave a disbelieving snort. '—For the *stability* of the airline,' she added firmly, 'it would be better if we ended the uncertainty of ownership as soon as possible.'

Blue eyes raked over her scathingly. 'You can't wait to crawl into his bed, can you?'

Heather paled at the viciousnesss of the taunt, all the more hurtful because it was the truth. When Daniel had asked her earlier if she were willing to share his bed, to give herself to him, she had known a thrill of anticipation like never before. She could imagine nothing more wonderful than being his woman. But it was his wife she was destined to be, a wife he was forced to accept, and not his woman at all.

Her eyes flashed as she glared at her aunt. 'I think our sleeping arrangement once we're married will be no one's concern but our own——'

'Or *before* we're married,' drawled Daniel as he suddenly appeared at her side, his arm moving possessively about her waist, his flinty gaze fixed on Stella's flushed face. 'Don't you know better than to taunt children? he jeered softly.

Stella relaxed a little, glancing dismissively at Heather. 'That *child* will be your wife in a month's time!'

He gave an acknowledging inclination of his head. 'As Heather has already said, we don't believe that is any of your business.'

Stella gave him a taunting smile. 'I suppose you should be admired, really,' she mocked.

'You——'

'Heather, I've performed all the duty dances that I'm going to,' he firmly cut in on her angry outburst, letting the other woman know that was all he considered his dance with *her* to be. 'When are we going to throw this lot out so that we can be alone?'

Lionel chuckled softly, obviously relieved to have someone step in and prevent the two women from indulging in a full-scale battle. 'I think that's a hint for us to make the first move to leave,' he told his wife indulgently.

'I can't imagine why the two of you would *want* to be alone,' Stella remarked, determined to be the one to have the last word.

Daniel looked at her with flinty eyes, before turning pointedly to Heather's alluring curves outlined in the clinging black dress, and then back again to the more obviously displayed charms of the older woman in the low-cut red dress. 'Can't you?' he taunted softly. 'I'm sure all the men in this room could give you numerous reasons!'

Strange as it felt, Heather was grateful for Daniel's defence of her, especially when Stella flounced off in search of her wrap, her chuckling husband following once he had kissed Heather warmly on the cheek and shaken Daniel by the hand. It was the first time that any man, with the exception of Uncle Lionel, had defended her in that way, and it felt a little strange to feel gratitude to a man who obviously held her in contempt.

Daniel shook his head as he watched the other couple leave, the expression on Stella's face boding ill for the older man once they were safely outside. 'I don't know how Lionel puts up with the shrew,' he muttered drily. 'If you turn into a witch like that I'll put you over my knee and spank you,' he warned harshly.

She stiffened, moving away from his arm about her waist. 'I'm grateful for your intervention just now,' she bit out abruptly. 'But I believe there are several things we need to discuss before we can be married.'

'Why do you think I want "rent-a-crowd" to leave?' he rasped. 'I want this thing settled, and I want it settled tonight!'

'Are you sure you can spare the time?' Her eyes flushed the colour of the flower she had been named for.

'Just,' he snapped grimly.

Her cheeks were flushed with anger at his arrogance, but she forced herself to relax as their guests took note of Lionel and Stella's departure, and came over to congratulate them one last time as they began to take their leave.

An hour later her cheeks ached from smiling so much, although she knew Daniel couldn't be suffering from the same affliction, his goodbyes terse to say the least. But finally the last guests had taken their leave, and they were now free to leave the staff to clear up the debris of the party while they retired to the small sitting-room where coffee was waiting for them.

Heather handed Daniel a cup of the black, unsweetened coffee she knew he preferred, watching as he curled a hand around the cup to take a sip, completely ignoring the delicate handle. Considering how hot the coffee had been when she poured it out, she was surprised he hadn't burnt his mouth. Although from his grim expression, he wouldn't have noticed even if he had!

He stood across the room from her, his rest-lessness something to be sensed, as he stood completely unmoving. 'Well?' he suddenly rasped.

Her hand shook slightly, spilling some of her coffee into the saucer. She didn't pretend to misunderstand what he meant. 'Well, fortu-

nately, although my father took care of the idea
of divorce—' the shares were to be sold and the
money distributed to the various charities,
exactly as it would have been if she didn't marry
Daniel! '—he didn't say anything about us
having to have a *normal* marriage——'

'In other words, you would prefer to leave
things as they are?' he said drily.

'No, I wouldn't!' She swallowed hard at the
speculative raise of his eyebrows. 'I don't
like—like a Cassandra in your life.' She looked
away after having made the admission.

'A mistress, you mean?' he drawled.

'Is that really what she is?' Heather frowned.
'Not a lover, or—or girl-friend?'

'I go to her for only one reason,' he shrugged.
'So, what do you think?'

The other woman was his mistress! 'Everyone
must know that, and—and——'

'And you couldn't stand the humiliation of
people thinking you can't satisfy me in bed,' he
said mockingly. '*Can* you satisfy me in bed?'

How did she know; she had never *tried* to
satisfy a man anywhere! But Daniel seemed to
think Phillip had been the most recent in a long
line of lovers for her, and she wasn't about to
tell him that after the mess her mother had
made of her life, pregnant by one man but
marrying another, she wasn't about to take *any*
risk of getting pregnant without a husband
herself. Since meeting Daniel she had been glad
she hadn't fallen into the bed-hopping trap
many of her friends had just because it was

expected of them, for she knew that he was the only man she had ever wanted in that way.

She looked at him challengingly. 'Can you satisfy *me* in bed?'

His mouth twisted in the semblance of a smile. 'Would you like to find out?'

Her mouth suddenly went dry at the instant way he had accepted her challenge. 'I——'

'Maybe we *should* find out,' he suggested slowly, putting down his empty cup to advance on her as she pressed back against the sofa. 'After all——' he took the cup from her unresisting fingers '—we should know what we'll be getting from this marriage,' he added harshly.

The pressure of his body on hers forced her back on to the sofa, and her mouth was open in protest as his lips descended on hers.

She was lost from the first touch, groaning softly as his mouth moved over and against hers in insistent demand, her arms moving up about his neck as her fingers became entangled in the thickness of his hair, increasing the pressure of his mouth on hers.

She had dreamt about his kisses, longed for them, even as she told herself they would never be hers. But they could *all* be hers, if only she could please him now!

She arched into his hand as he cupped her breast through the thin material of her dress, his body feeling warm and inviting as her arms moved beneath his jacket for closer contact, their kisses becoming wild as she felt the urgency of his response, glorying in his hardness, knowing she *could* satisfy him.

Her hair became a silken curtain over her face as she turned her head, Daniel's mouth moving down her throat, his deft fingers sliding the zip down her back to pull her dress off one shoulder, baring a breast for his hungry mouth. As he suckled and pulled and nibbled it felt like a thousand tiny needles of pleasure melting her body to pliancy, his hand moving up her thigh beneath her dress now, moving higher and higher . . . !

She gasped at the warm rush between her thighs, pushing against him, groaning her frustration as his hand was suddenly removed, her breast a swollen ache as his mouth left her, too. She blinked up at him dazedly as he stood up, straightening his shirt and jacket.

She swallowed hard, feeling bereft, her body still aching for him. 'Why did you stop?' Her voice was husky with longing.

'I didn't think a sofa, in the middle of a house crowded with servants, was the right place to finish this,' he drawled dismissively.

'But I—we——'

'You,' he corrected hardily. 'I believe we just answered your question.'

The colour drained from her cheeks. 'But I thought you—too——'

Daniel looked down at her with mocking grey eyes. 'We've just proved that I can satisfy you,' he told her drily. 'The fact that I became aroused by your response is not the same thing.'

It wasn't? But——Heather pulled her dress

back into place as she realised her breast was
still bared to him, the nipple pouting hungrily
for the touch of his lips. 'You didn't exactly
seem to hate it,' she snapped in her humiliation,
sitting up, surprised to see that the minute hand
on her watch showed that only ten minutes had
elapsed since she had gone into his arms; in that
ten minutes her whole life had changed.

'I think we know enough now to give this
marriage a try,' he continued abruptly. 'What
do you think?'

It was as if their lovemaking had just been an
experiment, coldly thought out, coldly executed.
And maybe to Daniel it had been, but she could
never think of her fiery response to him in the
same unemotional way. 'No more Cassandras?'
she prompted softly.

His expression was mocking. 'Not initially,
anyway,' he agreed. 'We'll give it a couple of
months to see how we get on together before
making promises neither of us can keep. After
all, just now didn't really prove that much.'

Only that she forgot everything but him as
soon as he touched her! She would *make* it the
same way for him.

'All right,' she nodded. 'We'll—we'll be lovers
for two months after we're married and see
what happens.'

'Oh, I think we both know what will happen,
Heather,' he taunted crudely. 'It's just a question of one of us becoming bored with it
happening!'

She moistened her lips with the pink tip of

her tongue. 'Does that happen—to you, often?'

'All the time,' he answered uninterestedly, glancing at his watch. 'Why else do you think I've never married?'

She shrugged. 'Because you've never fallen in love.'

Daniel gave a disbelieving snort. 'Surely you realise that love is the last thing to come along in a relationship, that desire and wanting come first, and that more often than not once they have been satisfied love never rears its ugly head!'

'Ugly?' She swallowed at his description of the emotion that had caused her more pain than any other, but which she acknowledged had also enriched her life.

His eyes narrowed. 'It devours and dominates, makes you half a person. It's an emotion few can afford!'

She knew he was telling her that this was the reason for his success, that he had pushed love from his life to achieve the wealth and prestige he had wanted, and that he intended keeping it from his life. She felt a sinking feeling in her heart.

'And certainly not me,' he harshly confirmed her thoughts. 'We're being forced into this marriage by your father's will,' he told her with brutal honesty. 'Don't get any romantic ideas about me; they would be a complete waste of time!'

'Have many women dared to have "romantic ideas" about you?' she scorned to hide the pain his words caused, knowing that few women could feel romantic about this hardened man. She just happened to be one of the ones who did!

'I'm more accustomed to mercenary ones,' he conceded gratingly. 'I can live with them.'

Her eyes flashed. 'Your motives are no more innocent than mine!' she snapped.

'Then we start out as equals,' he drawled mockingly, again glancing at his watch. 'I think you were also concerned earlier about where we're going to live after the wedding?' He raised dark brows.

She should have known this sharp-eyed man wouldn't have missed her questioning glance in his direction when they were asked that. 'Where *are* we going to live?'

Daniel drew in a ragged breath. 'I have no intention of moving in here,' he told her challengingly.

Heather gave a nod of calm acceptance. 'Then we'll sell this house and find somewhere we both like——'

'You aren't going to argue about it?' He eyed her warily.

Her mouth quirked at his suspicious expression. 'Why should I?'

'Because you've lived in this house all your life.' He still watched her frowningly.

'Then it's time for a change,' she shrugged. 'I would like to take some of the staff with me, if that's all right with you?' She looked up at him enquiringly. 'The ones that have been with us the longest,' she explained. 'We wouldn't need all of them, because I think a smaller house would suit our needs better than this one. If you agree, of course?'

Daniel still watched her warily, as if she had suddenly become someone he didn't recognise. 'If *I* agree?' he echoed drily.

'Well, it's going to be *our* house, and——'

'You'll be spending the most time in it,' he cut in harshly. 'Buy as big a house as you want—or don't want. As long as I don't have to live *here* I don't care!' His eyes glittered coldly.

Heather blinked at his vehemence. 'Couldn't we choose somewhere together?'

'I told you, I won't be there that much—and not for the reason you're thinking,' he grated at her frown. 'I don't say things I don't mean, Heather, and if I've said I'll be faithful to you for at least the first two months of our marriage then I damn well will! I won't be at home much to start with because after the last damaging six months of uncertainty I'm going to have to work damned hard to rebuild the airline's reputation as a stable one!'

'I'm sorry,' she gave a guilty blush. 'I only——Couldn't I perhaps find two or three places I think might be suitable and then just show you them quickly one day? I promise not to take up too much of your time,' she added persuasively.

He looked irritated. 'Don't try and make me feel guilty because I have to try and correct the damage *your* father did to——'

'I wasn't,' she assured him quickly, feeling as if she had to walk on eggshells around this man. 'Daniel, are you sure you're going to be able to cope with the tie of a wife?'

'No, I'm not sure at all.' His eyes glittered. 'But neither of us has a choice!'

She could already see how he was chafing at having to explain even the most impersonal of things to her, and wondered what it would be like once they were married.

But he was wrong about the choice; she *did* have one. It was just one she knew she could never take, not when it meant hurting Daniel so much.

'Daniel, I'm as upset about my father's will as you are,' she began.

'Oh, I realise that,' he derided. 'I'm sure you expected to walk away with a fortune, not a husband as well! I know why Max hated me; I just wonder what you ever did to him!'

She turned away to hide the pain in her clouded eyes. 'He wanted a son; he got me.' She flatly told him the half-truth, the wound of Max Danvers' rejection, although an old one, still raw.

'And he wanted money but instead he got *me,*' Daniel rasped harshly. 'And now, it seems, we have each other!'

Even now, loving him as she did, she wished there were something she could do to release him from the tie to her that he didn't want. But there was nothing she could do.

She sighed. 'I'll try not to be intrusive on your life in any way.'

'I never wanted a wife!' he exclaimed with impatient anger.

'I promise you——'

'Don't make me any promises, Heather,' he scorned. 'Women are notorious for breaking them!'

She would like to think, much as it would also pain her, that he had once cared enough for a woman to have been hurt by her; at least then she could have some hope that he was capable of love! But she was sure that wasn't how he had come to his biased conclusion concerning women, he didn't seem to care for *anyone*.

'Then only time will show you that I mean what I say,' she sighed. 'I'll intrude on your life and time as little as possible.'

'Except to look at houses, to no doubt help shop for furniture for that house, to dictate that there will be no other women in my life——'

'You dictated that there shouldn't be any other men in mine,' she retorted fierily, her tempestuous nature not completely cowed by her efforts to reassure him. 'I retain the right to make the same conditions over you.'

'For two months,' he reminded her grimly.

An angry blush darkened her cheeks. 'I'm sure it will pass quickly—for both of us.'

'I hope so!'

Heather sighed. 'You aren't giving this relationship a chance if you're going to be counting

the days until you can go back to your
mistress——Why do you keep looking at your
watch?' she demanded impatiently as he glanced
at it for the third time in the last ten minutes.

His mouth twisted with cruel mockery. 'We
aren't married yet!'

'I only asked——' She broke off, looking at
him closely as his meaning suddenly became
crystal clear. 'Do you have—somewhere else to
go tonight?' she queried haltingly, wishing it not
to be true.

'Yes,' he rasped with satisfaction.

She swallowed hard, knowing exactly where
that 'somewhere else' was—to his mistress,
Cassandra! But as he had so viciously pointed
out, they weren't married yet, and even if they
were, she doubted he would particularly care if
he humiliated her; he hated her because he had
been trapped into marrying her.

'Do you have to go to her tonight?' she
frowned.

He shrugged broad shoulders. 'Why not?'

'I——You could always stay here instead.'
Her eyes were wide with apprehension—and
anticipation!

'Thanks for the offer,' he derided. 'But in a
month's time I'm not going to have a choice
about who I share my bed—and my body with;
right now, I do!'

Heather flinched as if he had hit her. She
hadn't made the suggestion lightly, she just
hated the thought of him going to the other
woman! But she could see by the satisfied gleam

in Daniel's eyes that he was enjoying hurting her, that he had far from forgiven her for her involvement in this enforced marriage. As if she would have wanted him as her husband in this way, given a choice!

'In that case, I have the same choice,' she retaliated lightly. 'And it isn't too late to give—a friend a call.

Daniel's eyes narrowed to icy grey slits. 'Wingate?' he scorned.

'Perhaps,' she said non-committally, standing up. 'I really shouldn't keep you any longer . . . ' she added pointedly.

'My, you are in a hurry to finish what we started earlier, aren't you?' he taunted, following her out into the hallway.

She stood her ground without blushing —much as her cheeks burned! 'No more so than you appear to be,' she mocked.

He halted at the front door. 'If I hadn't told Cassandra that I would see her tonight . . . ' He trailed off softly.

'I wouldn't want you to disappoint her,' Heather snapped angrily, holding the door open, all the household staff still busy in the main lounge.

'No,' he sighed, one of his hands moving to lightly caress her cheek with his thumb-pad. 'Perhaps anticipation will be good for the soul,' he taunted. 'It seems that the wedding night I thought would be such an ordeal won't be so bad after all!'

Before Heather could come back with a suitably cutting retort he had walked off into the darkness, his chuckle at her speechlessness carrying to her on the night air.

She closed the door with a slam. Damn him, he had almost made her beg for what he now admitted he had anticipated with dread! He——

She turned sharply as the doorbell rang. If he thought he could come back and change his mind *now* he was sadly mistaken!

'Phillip!' she gasped, after furiously wrenching the door open. She had told Daniel she intended calling the other man, but really Phillip was the last person she had expected to see again tonight!

CHAPTER THREE

'CAN I come in?' Phillip prompted softly, as Heather continued to stare at him in astonishment.

'I——Of course,' she invited abruptly. After the way he had walked out earlier she hadn't expected to see him again at all, let alone now!

She led the way to the small sitting-room, facing him awkwardly. 'It's late,' she said unnecessarily; they were both aware of the fact that it was one o'clock in the morning. 'Daniel just left,' she added uncomfortably, as she saw his gaze linger on the two empty coffee cups.

'I know.' His hair was golden in the glow of the overhead chandelier. 'I saw him leave. In fact, I deliberately waited until he'd gone before ringing the bell.'

She frowned at this disclosure. 'You did?'

'Hm,' Phillip nodded, his expression rueful. 'I wanted to apologise for my behaviour earlier, and I didn't particularly want to have to do it in front of Taggart.' His deep blue eyes had hardened a little as he spoke of the other man, his good looks in no doubt, his features almost too perfect for a man, his body lithe and attractive in the dark evening suit.

'I understood earlier why you felt you had to

leave,' she sighed. 'All this has been very awkward for you.'

'Worse than that,' he groaned. 'Heather, I love you, and it's killing me to see you preparing to marry another man!'

They had been close the last year, good friends, occasionally a little more than that, but only a *little* more; she liked to be kissed and held as much as the next person. But she had never expected a declaration of love from him, it just hadn't been that sort of a relationship. At least, not as far as she was concerned.

'I'm sorry, Phillip,' she sounded breathless, 'your friendship has meant a lot to me——'

'Friendship!' he repeated scornfully. 'You had to realise I was falling in love with you!'

Had she? They had seen each other a couple of times a week, enjoyed each other's company, occasionally shared a few pleasant kisses, but did that mean a man was falling in love with her. She hadn't thought so, had imagined being swept away in a maelstrom of wild emotions —much like she had known in Daniel's arms such a short time ago!—when she loved, not feel the warmth of friendship.

'I didn't, Phillip,' she told him truthfully. 'I just thought we liked each other.'

He looked angry. 'But you can't be in love with a man like Taggart!'

She stiffened at the condescension he obviously felt for the man who employed him. 'Why can't I?'

'Because you're soft, and beautiful, totally

lovable—and he's a callous bastard!' Phillip
rasped harshly. 'He isn't capable of loving
anyone!'

Maybe Phillip was right about the latter, but
she didn't believe Daniel was callous. He was
hard, afraid to love in case he got hurt, but he
only hit out at others to protect himself, not for
the sake of it. She was an expert on callous
men, had lived with one for twenty years, and
Daniel wasn't one of them.

'You're talking about the man I intend to
marry,' she reminded her coolly.

'You can't marry *him!*'

'Daniel and I intend being married in four
weeks——'

'Four weeks?' Phillip echoed incredulously.
'My God, he isn't taking any chances on you
changing your mind, is he?' he scorned.

Heather shook her head, her gaze flinty. 'I
won't change my mind, no matter how many
weeks it is until we get married.'

His eyes narrowed disbelievingly. 'You love
him?'

It was one thing to admit the emotion to
herself, something else completely to admit the
feeling to someone else. 'I'm marrying him,' she
insisted tightly. 'Now, it's late, Phillip, and
I——'

'Everyone will know he's only marrying you
because of the airline!'

She was suddenly still, looking at him sharply.
'What do you mean?'

He shrugged, his gaze not quite meeting hers.

'It has to be obvious to anyone with even half a brain,' he bit out impatiently. 'You inherited your father's share of Air International, and so Taggart has decided to marry you!'

She relaxed a little, confident he knew nothing about the full details of her father's will, that he had no idea both she and Daniel were being pressured into the marriage. 'Is that what everyone thought tonight?' she frowned.

'Well, none of them are going to say it to your face——'

'Why not? You did!'

He sighed, lightly clasping her shoulders, his eyes compassionate. 'Because I care for you, because I don't want to see Taggart making a fool of you.'

'And why do you think *I'm* marrying him?' she prompted softly.

He shook his head. 'I don't know, but I do know you can't be in love with him. Call off the wedding, Heather, and marry me!'

She moved pointedly out of his arms. 'I'm engaged to Daniel.'

'You don't wear his ring!' Phillip pounced.

Because so far Daniel hadn't found the time to shop for one, and she was damned if she was going to go out and buy her own engagement ring! 'We have a verbal agreement,' she insisted firmly. 'We don't need a ring to make it official.'

Phillip's shoulders dropped dejectedly. 'You do love him,' he realised heavily.

'I'm sorry if you've been hurt.' She didn't confirm or deny his statement; Daniel wouldn't hear from a third person that she had admitted to loving him!

'Are you?' Phillip scorned disbelievingly.

'Phillip, please——'

'Please, what?' he sighed, putting a hand over his eyes. 'Oh, God, I came here to tell you how much I love you and I end up arguing with you!' He looked at her with pained eyes. 'Forgive me, Heather.'

She felt as if all this were her fault, as if she must have encouraged him to believe his feelings were returned. 'Of course,' she soothed, her hand consolingly on his arm. 'I really never meant to hurt you.'

'I know that,' he said heavily. 'I just expected too much.'

'I—Uncle Lionel said something about sending you up to Manchester for a while, maybe in the circumstances that would be best——'

'No,' he refused harshly, his expression softening as he saw her startled expression. 'I'll behave, Heather, you don't have to send me away like a naughty little boy,' he rasped.

'Uncle Lionel was only doing what he thought best——'

'If I promise not to make a nuisance of myself, even to come to your wedding, will you ask him to reconsider?' Phillip persuaded.

'What's so wrong with Manchester that everyone tries to avoid going there?' she attempted to tease, sensing the tension of the moment was passing.

'Speaking for myself, nothing,' he drawled. 'I just happen to prefer London.'

'Then I'll talk to Uncle Lionel,' she agreed lightly. 'I'm sure they can really do with you down here for the moment.'

'Things *are* a little hectic,' he acknowledged drily. 'But maybe that will change now.'

She raised dark brows in innocent enquiry. 'Oh?'

'I'm sure your uncle—and Taggart, must have told you about the interest Public Airlines have been showing in the airline since your father died,' Phillip drawled. 'Now that you and Taggart are banding together the airline will be more solid than it ever has been before,' he added scornfully.

Heather was well aware of the larger airline's interest in Air International, it was one of the main reasons she and Daniel had decided to end all the speculation now and announce their engagement. Obviously, Phillip wouldn't be the only one to draw the correct conclusion, and she knew that, despite the success of the party tonight and the good wishes, the next few months were going to be difficult ones. But she had succeeded for years in appearing like Max Danvers' pride and joy in public while being scorned by him in private, surely it couldn't be that much harder to appear like Daniel's joyful wife?

'I never thought of it that way,' she remarked lightly.

'I'll bet Taggart has,' he rasped tightly. 'I'm

sorry, Heather,' he sighed as anger flared in her eyes. 'But I hate the thought of his marrying you for what he can get out of it!'

'The only thing Daniel will be "getting" out of this marriage, Phillip, is me,' she told him softly. 'I'll still maintain control of my share of the company.'

'Under his guidance,' he derided. 'You know absolutely nothing about running an airline—or if it's being run properly!'

That was true; her father hadn't believed in women in business, especially *his* business. The qualifications she had been allowed to gain on leaving school had remained unused, at her father's request. He had wanted her as the hostess of his home, and because she had still been trying to find a way to make him love her she had agreed to put her own dreams aside.

Her sacrifice had been in vain, but years of pleasing the man who despised her were difficult to dispel, and so she had become the social butterfly Max wanted—and which Daniel obviously despised. Maybe now would be the right time to think about the career she had always wanted, although it *wouldn't* be at Air International.

She trusted Daniel to do what he thought best for the airline, knew that they had to trust each other if this marriage was to stand a chance of survival. And it would survive, because she was in love with him, and surely that had to count for something. Didn't it . . . ?

'But Daniel and my uncle *do* know,' she

dismissed lightly. 'You really have no need to worry about me, Phillip, I do know what I'm doing!'

He gave a defeated sigh in the face of her certainty. 'If ever you *do* need a friend, for whatever reason, I want you to know you can call on me.'

'I do.' She gave him a warm smile. 'But I'm sure everything is going to work out just fine.'

Her sleepless night belied her confidence —and this was only the start!

'There's a gentleman to see you, Miss Heather,' Shilton, the family butler for as long as she could remember, informed her the next morning. 'He says his name is Ronaldway,' he supplied. 'And that Mr Taggart sent him here.'

Heather looked up from the bridal designs she had been going through all morning —without success. None of the gowns was what she wanted to walk down the aisle to Daniel in. This gown had to be something special. She knew she was being picky, that every bride probably felt the same way about their own wedding gown, but most of those brides would be confident of their groom's love, know that he would think them beautiful whatever they wore. She didn't have that reassurance.

She put the designs to one side, frowning up at Shilton. 'Did he say what he wanted?'

'No,' he replied drily.

Heather gave a brief smile as she sensed his

disapproval of the other man's reticence. 'Then
you'd better show him in,' she requested lightly.
'And perhaps you could organise some
coffee . . . ?'

'Of course, Miss Heather.' He gave a haughty
nod.

She was still smiling to herself when he showed
the other man in; really, Shilton was more of a
snob than her father had been! But, for all that,
she was fond of the now elderly man, hoping
he would be one of the staff that moved with
her once she and Daniel had found their own
house.

She stood up, holding out her hand to the
impeccably dressed man, small and wiry, with
sparse brown hair. 'Mr Ronaldway,' she greeted
warmly. 'How may I help you?'

'It's I who may serve you,' he corrected
politely, his dark brown eyes rather speculative,
as if she weren't quite what he had been
expecting of Heather Danvers.

His surprise caused her to question her own
appearance, but she knew there was nothing
wrong with the purple trousers and pale lilac
silk blouse; that the former perfectly matched
her eyes, the latter complemented the darkness
of her hair. Maybe she was just imagining things,
felt sensitive because Daniel had sent the man
here.

'Oh?' she prompted smoothly.

'Yes, indeed.' He placed the briefcase he had
been carrying when he entered the room on top
of the coffee-table, clicking open the locks. 'Mr

Taggart discussed preferences with me on the telephone, and on that basis I believe one of the outstanding collection of rings I have brought with me should meet your approval.'

Even as the words 'preferences' and 'telephone' and 'rings' penetrated Heather's brain the man beside her had removed several velvet trays from within the briefcase, each tray presenting three diamond rings, their combined brilliance dazzling her.

Henry Ronaldway smiled proudly at her speechlessness. 'They are lovely, aren't they?' he beamed.

All of them were beautiful, diamond clusters, solitaires, a lovers' knot. And Heather knew that one of them was supposed to be her engagement ring. Now she understood the man's surprise when he first arrived; she hadn't been at all what he had expected the fiancée of Daniel Taggart to be! A cold anger settled in her chest and remained there.

'They are very beautiful, Mr Ronaldway,' she assured him distantly. 'Unfortunately, there seems to have been some confusion about the time you were to call; I'm afraid my fiancé is unavailable this morning.'

His smile faltered and faded. 'Oh, but I understood from Mr Taggart——'

She knew exactly what he had 'understood' from Daniel! 'Could you possibly come back some other time?' She moved pointedly towards the door as she spoke. 'I'll have—Mr Taggart call you when it's convenient for us both.'

'There's nothing wrong, is there, Miss Danvers?' He frowned worriedly, obviously concerned he might be losing the sale.

'Nothing at all.' She gave him a blinding smile. 'I'm sure you can understand that my fiancé and I would like to choose the ring together.'

He had carefully repacked the rings into the briefcase now, still looking puzzled. 'But Mr Taggart explained to me that he wouldn't be here, that——'

'Whatever he told you I'm sure you must have misunderstood him, Mr Ronaldway,' she cut in firmly. 'And, until Mr Taggart tells you he *is* available, your visit is not convenient.' She looked at him challengingly.

The man she watched leave the house seconds later was far from the happy one he had been when he arrived!

How *could* Daniel! How dared he send some jeweller over here, a man he had merely spoken to on the *telephone,* that he hadn't even spoken to in *person,* with the intention of her picking out her engagement ring on her own?

Admittedly, the rings had been beautiful, he had obviously spared no expense in his selections, but she would rather not have a ring at all if it meant she had to choose one alone. And Daniel had a nerve believing that she would! He couldn't have shown her any more clearly how contemptuous he was of their engagement.

'I won't be needing that now, thank you,' she told the maid stiltedly as she came in with a

tray of coffee, coming to an abrupt decision.
'I'm going out!' She ran up to her room to
collect her jacket, the weather being decidedly
cool for August. Not that she felt the same way,
her temper raging out of control.

It became worse, not better, as she drove to
the company's head office. How dared Daniel
insult her in that way, sending over a dozen
rings for her to choose from, imagining that she
would meekly accept the condescension! She
wasn't *that* worried about wearing his ring!

'I'm afraid Mr Taggart isn't here at the
moment,' Gloria, his secretary, told her regretfully after she had burst into his office asking to
see him.

The other woman had been her father's
secretary until his death six months ago, and
Heather knew her quite well; she should have
thought to call Gloria to make sure of Daniel's
presence in his office before speeding over here!
'When do you expect him back?' she asked
irritably.

Gloria grimaced her uncertainty. 'I'm not
really sure. Mr Taggart likes his time to be
flexible.'

Not flexible enough that he could spare five
minutes to help choose her engagement ring!
'OK, thanks,' Heather sighed. 'I have to see my
uncle about something, anyway, I'll check back
with you before I leave.'

'Congratulations on your engagement to Mr
Taggart, Miss Danvers,' the other woman said
warmly as Heather turned to leave.

Congratulations on becoming engaged to a
selfish, arrogant—my God, she thought, Gloria
probably knew all about the Cassandras in
Daniel's life, probably took telephone calls and
messages from them all the time! 'Thank you,'
she accepted stiffly, her head held high as she
went in search of her uncle.

She rarely came to the offices of Air International, accepting that she *didn't* know how to
run an airline, and respecting the fact that her
uncle and Daniel did. But she knew her way
around well enough, greeting her uncle's
secretary with a friendly smile.

'I'll just tell him you're here.' Lynn returned
the smile. 'I must just tell you how excited we
all are about your engagement to Mr Taggart,'
she added breathlessly.

And they hadn't even put the announcement
in *The Times* yet; at this rate they wouldn't need
to bother! 'Thank you,' Heather accepted drily.

'Heather!' Her uncle came out to greet her as
soon as he had been informed of her arrival,
clasping her hands in his. 'It's lovely to see you,'
he told her as they went through to his luxuri-
ously appointed office. 'You're looking radiant
this morning.'

She was still so angry she didn't know how
she looked. 'I hope you didn't mind my tele-
phoning you earlier.' She sat down opposite
him, crossing one trouser-covered leg over the
other.

'Of course not,' he instantly reassured her.
'Phillip is one young man I would rather not do

without at the moment if I don't have to.'

She had called him first thing this morning and requested that he not send Phillip to Manchester, assuring him that everything was fine between her and Phillip now. She wasn't quite sure that was true, but it didn't seem fair that Phillip should have to take responsibility for the awkwardness between them.

'Good,' she nodded.

'Besides,' he added teasingly, 'this is half your airline, you know.'

She gave a deep sigh. 'You'll never know how much I wish it weren't.'

He frowned. 'Did you and Daniel have an argument after we all left last night?'

She gave him a frowning look. 'What makes you say that?' she mused.

'Well, you seem a little—agitated today, and Daniel has been snarling at everyone all morning. I didn't think the two could be a coincidence!'

But they were. Heather's anger evaporated somewhat as she envisaged trouble with Cassandra because of his lateness last night as the reason for Daniel's bad humour. It would serve him right if the other woman was coming to the conclusion that she didn't like the idea of him having a wife!

'*Did* you have an argument?' her uncle probed concernedly.

'No more than usual,' she dismissed lightly. 'This marriage is going to be a battlefield!' But at least it wouldn't be dull, she acknowledged

to herself, feeling decidedly more cheerful now
that she knew of Daniel's ill humour.

Her uncle laughed softly. 'You sound as if
you're looking forward to it.'

Heather smiled. 'I think I am!'

'As long as you're happy,' her uncle nodded.
'How about joining me for lunch? It's just about
that time.'

'I'd love to,' she accepted, suddenly feeling
much more light-hearted. She could sort out the
problem of the ring later.

She was just telling her uncle about her dissat-
isfaction with the dress designs she had so far
looked at, when the lift doors opened and Daniel
and Stella stepped out, so deep in conversation
they didn't notice Heather and Lionel at first.
Heather was so startled to see the other two
together that she just gaped at them in amazement.

Stella was the first to recover from the tableau.
'Look who I met outside!' She kissed her
husband on the cheek.

Heather looked suspiciously at the other
woman; had her words been just a little too
forced, the explanation for her and Daniel being
together just a little too lightly given to be
genuine? She couldn't exactly see Daniel and
Stella involved in an affair, and there was Uncle
Lionel and Cassandra to consider too, and yet
the memory of the other couple dancing closely
together the previous evening persisted.

'Heather and I were just on our way out to
lunch,' Lionel supplied lightly.

'And I was just on my way to invite you to join *me* for lunch,' Stella pouted her disappointment.

'No problem,' drawled Daniel, speaking for the first time since he had stepped out of the lift, his flinty gaze fixed on Heather. 'Why don't you join Lionel, Stella? Heather and I have a few things to discuss anyway.'

Heather gave him a wary look, not liking his tone of voice at all. And then she remembered her own anger towards him, her eyes sparkling with challenge. 'Yes, the two of you go ahead,' she invited. 'Daniel and I have several things to—talk over.'

Grey eyes narrowed at her own significant pause, Daniel's fingers were steely on her arm as he guided her to his office, nodding tersely to Gloria as he waited impatiently for Heather to precede him into the room.

She couldn't remember ever having been in Daniel's office before, but the large furniture and austere décor were exactly what she would have expected of him; it matched his personality, dark and unrevealing.

She faced him boldly as he sat behind the wide mahogany desk, not at all intimidated by the coldness in his eyes. 'Are you sure you have the time now for this discussion?' she scorned angrily. 'I thought you were supposed to be very busy today.'

'Did you?' he returned softly.

'Yes,' she snapped, her eyes flashing a warning.

He shrugged. 'Even I have to eat, and this happens to be my lunch break.'

'I suppose I should be flattered that you want to waste any of it on me!' Her eyes glittered.

Daniel's expression darkened. 'I don't know what the hell's got into you today——'

'Don't you?' she challenged brittly, sitting opposite him now. 'Perhaps the name Ronaldway will jog your memory!'

Grey eyes narrowed, flickering to the nakedness of her left hand. 'If you didn't like the rings he showed you this morning I'm sure he has others. I thought you would like the diamonds, but if there's some other stone that you prefer——'

'I'd *prefer* it if we chose the ring together, not have you telephone your orders through as if you were ordering room service!' Heather's cheeks were flushed with anger, and she was breathing deeply in her agitation.

'Not at all,' Daniel drawled. 'I'm very particular about the food I eat!'

Heather stood up, shaking with the force of her anger. 'You arrogant son-of-a——'

'My mother wasn't a bitch.' Daniel had stood up to move around his desk, catching her wrist as she would have struck him, his eyes glittering dangerously. 'She was a little stupid, more than a little naïve, but pleasant none the less. Now, if you had called me a bastard it would have been a different matter,' he rasped. 'Because that's indisputably what I am. "Father unknown", I believe it says on my birth certificate!'

Her anger left her as suddenly as it had flared up, sure he knew exactly what it said on his birth certificate. They had so much in common, she and this man who hid the pain of his fatherless background behind a veneer of coldness. Oh, she had known who her father was, she had been told by her mother of his death in a car accident when Heather was only five years old. But both of them had grown up without a father's love.

'Don't pity me!' Daniel thrust her away from him as he correctly read the compassion on her face. 'As you can see, I've done very well without knowing my father!'

He had done well to *spite* his father—whoever he was. She could see it in his face now, his wealth a challenge to the man who hadn't cared enough to be his father. It was as if he were saying, 'Am I good enough for you to know *now?*'

'You're a clever man, Daniel,' she admitted softly. 'But not clever enough,' she added boldly, 'to know that I would rather not wear your ring at all than have you send over a batch for me to choose from as if it were a new dress, or something equally as unimportant!'

'It's only a ring, Heather, a symbol of ownership, not love,' he dismissed scathingly.

But it was so much more than that to her! Oh, what was the use? Daniel didn't love her, he would never understand how important wearing his ring had seemed to her.

'Then maybe we shouldn't bother with——'

'The marriage?' he finished erroneously. 'Did your lover persuade you to continue to fight the will, after all?' he scorned.

Her cheeks were flushed, his fingers biting into her wrist where he still held her. 'I was going to say, not bother with an engagement ring,' she corrected impatiently. 'It seems to mean so little to you, it hardly seems worth the effort. What lover?' She frowned.

'Wingate!' he dismissed harshly. 'I think I should tell you here and now that, although this airline may be half yours, I do not appreciate your intervention in management decisions concerning members of the staff—even if you're sleeping with the member of staff in question. *Especially* if you're sleeping with the member of staff in question!' he added grimly.

Heather's eyes were dark purple in her pale face. 'You're talking about Phillip?' she prompted incredulously.

'Of course I'm "talking about Phillip",' he mimicked cruelly, thrusting her disgustedly away from him. 'Last night, you and Lionel decided to move Wingate up to Manchester for a while so that he could get over his disappointment at not being chosen as your groom,' he scorned. 'After sharing your bed with him for the night, and when Lionel had already begun to put the proposal in action, *you* called him and told him you don't think it's necessary after all!' His eyes glittered.

'That isn't the way it happened——'

'Did you see Wingate after I left you last night?' Daniel cut in harshly.

The colour came—and then went, in her cheeks. 'Well—yes. He did come to see me. But not——'

'And he persuaded you to give him a reprieve about Manchester,' Daniel accused disgustedly. 'Is that all it takes to get your compliance, a night in your bed?' His flinty gaze raked over her contemptuously.

'You're being unfair——'

'I'm warning the woman who's about to become *my* wife that you'd better be damned sure you know what you're doing when you go through with the wedding next month,' he told her harshly. 'Because once you *are* my wife, only death will free you!'

'Daniel!' she groaned weakly, a shiver of apprehension running down her spine.

'Oh, get out of here!' He moved away from her with disgust. 'Enjoy your pretty lover in your bed for the next four weeks. But make damn sure I never find him in *our* bed after that time. I'd break his damned neck for him!'

Heather looked at his bent head as he sat down to study some papers on the top of his desk, sure that he meant every word that he said. He *was* capable of physical violence if the occasion warranted it.

When she had telephoned her uncle this morning she had had no way of knowing he had already discussed the move to Manchester for Phillip with Daniel, although she realised now that as one of the airline's top executives Phillip couldn't be sent to the other office *without* clearing it with Daniel first. She should have known that, and the construction Daniel would put on her request that they forget about the idea. But at the time, she had just thought she was helping a friend, not stirring up this hornets' nest. And she didn't know what she could say to undo the damage she had already done, except to tell Daniel that Phillip wasn't her lover, and he had already made it obvious he wasn't going to believe *that*.

Glacial grey eyes raked into her as Daniel suddenly looked up. 'Still here?' he taunted, sitting back in his plush leather chair. 'I thought you would have hurried off by now to make the most of the time you have left to spend with your lover!'

She drew in an angry breath. 'I'm not even going to try and justify myself to you just now,' she snapped. 'You obviously——'

'That's good,' he drawled before she could finish speaking. 'I doubt that you could, anyway,' he added derisively.

'Oh, I can, believe me.' She trembled as she thought of the shock he was going to receive on their wedding night. 'But, right now, I don't intend to.'

'Of course not,' he mocked.

Her eyes flashed. 'You don't think I can, do you?'

He shrugged. 'What does it matter what I

think?' he dismissed. 'You have yourself a bride-groom, the wedding takes place in four weeks, and for two months after that we try to remain faithful to each other. What else do I need to know?'

'Nothing,' she bit out; he made it sound as if she had *bought* herself a bridegroom. He bene-fited as much as she did by this marriage, more if you considered that she was also gaining a husband she loved but who didn't love her!

'I'll see you in church on the twenty-fifth,' he nodded abruptly.

Heather turned and left, her head held high. She wasn't as easily dismissed as he thought, and he would soon learn that!

CHAPTER FOUR

'—Now speak, or else hereafter for ever hold his peace.' The vicar paused only briefly, and yet Heather felt herself tense, her breath held expectantly.

The last four weeks had been busy, so many things to organise, not least of them being the sale of the old house and the acquisition of the new one, that the time had sped by so fast Heather hadn't had time to know what day it was, let alone dwell on the consequences of what she was doing marrying Daniel at all.

But now she did, and she realised that there were at least three other people in the church, besides Daniel and herself, who knew that they were marrying each other for all the wrong reasons; Uncle Lionel and Stella, and her father's —and now her own—lawyer.

Why didn't any of them speak up, she thought a little hysterically, denounce this marriage as a sham? Why didn't *she?* This marriage was a travesty, an insult to the vows she and Daniel were about to make to each other. Someone should stop it! Why didn't——

She gave a nervous start of surprise as she felt Daniel's fingers glide caressingly down her arm to become entwined with her own, soothing her, calming the hysteria in her more effectively than any words could have done.

She blinked up at him, unaware of how pale she had suddenly become. The warmth in his eyes made her heart leap, beating faster as she became mesmerised by his powerful presence, reciting her vows huskily when the time came.

She loved this man, would be a good wife to him, whether he wanted her to be or not. Oh, she knew he didn't love her, but maybe he could learn, in time.

They had been together a lot the last month. Daniel might not have *wanted* to see her again, until they stood side by side today, when she had left his office all those weeks ago, but once their engagement became public knowledge they had received numerous invitations, and Daniel had been forced to accompany her to at least some of them. He was still the same man that mocked her and all her friends but, over the weeks, they had at least learnt to relax a little in each other's company.

Until today! Today Heather had left her bed with the knowledge that before she returned to it she would be Daniel's wife, that he would be sharing it with her, for at least part of the night. Their new house, the house they had finally chosen together, wouldn't be ready to move into for another week, and so, as Daniel couldn't get away just now, they were being forced to spend the next week in her father's house. It was far from an ideal arrangement, but they could hardly move into a hotel when their house was in town.

God, how she was dreading tonight! She would be making love with a stranger. She loved Daniel—was sure, after loving him all this time, that she always would—but the limit of her experience with men could be written on a postage stamp, and Daniel was used to experience from his bed-partners. As the wedding—and consequently the wedding night —had loomed nearer, she had changed her mind about Daniel being surprised when he realised she was a virgin, and had instead decided he was more likely to be disappointed. She very much doubted he would relish the idea of initiating an innocent. She knew it wasn't going to be easy to accomplish, but she was going to try and make sure he didn't *get* an innocent!

The formalities over, the register signed, in no time at all they were walking back down the aisle as husband and wife.

Heather Taggart. She was now Mrs Daniel Taggart. She had loved him for so long, and so helplessly, that she had never dreamt this day would come. And for all the wrong reasons. But other marriages had started with less and been a success, her mother's marriage to Max had been one of them. He might have disliked Heather, but she had never doubted his true affection for her mother, knew of the deep love he had had for her when he was devastated by her death. And if that marriage could survive against all the odds, maybe this one could, too!

Daniel sat grimly beside her in the white limousine that had been hired especially for the occasion, as they were driven to the reception that was being held for them at one of London's leading hotels.

He had hated this wedding and all it stood for, Heather could see that from his expression, blinking back the threatening tears as she watched him brush confetti and rice from his hair with barely concealed impatience. And the dress she had chosen with such care, its Regency style and her loosely upswept hair suiting her perfectly, might have been a sack for all the notice he had taken of it, his expression being one of resignation rather than happiness as she walked down the aisle as his bride.

'Never mind, Daniel,' she bit out bitterly, drawing his attention from out of the window to her. 'Only another few hours of this and you can consider your duty as my husband done!'

'Really?' He arched dark brows. 'I thought I had one more duty to perform!'

And he didn't mean partnering her during the first dance at the reception! 'If our wedding night is so distasteful to you——'

'Oh, it isn't,' he said softly, suddenly very close, the length of his thigh resting against hers, burning through the chiffon of her dress. 'We have yet to find out if you can arouse *me!*'

'Daniel——'

'Hm?' he murmured distractedly, his mouth against the base of her throat. 'I like your dress, by the way,' he told her huskily, barely allowing her to feel warmed by the compliment before adding, 'It allows me to see what I'm getting!'

She gasped her indignation, moving as far away from him on the leather seat as she could, returning his amused gaze with a fierce glare. The Regency style was more popularly known for its high waist, but the neckline was cut quite low too, and the material was very sheer. She had chosen to wear tiny white roses in her hair instead of a veil, and so she didn't even have that to pull defensively about her in the face of his insulting tone.

Her mouth was set tightly. 'Every other man at the wedding can see what you're "getting", too,' she challenged snappily.

Daniel relaxed back on his side of the seat. 'Ah, but most of them have already had it!' he drawled softly.

Heather was left speechless at the insult. She wouldn't give him the *satisfaction* of knowing he was her first lover!

'But not like I'm going to,' he added audaciously, his eyes flinty as his gaze swept over her from head to toe, leaving Heather in no doubt of his intent to know every inch of her. 'We should make beautiful children together,' he drawled derisively.

Children! He wanted *children?* With *her?* 'We've never talked about—having a family?' Her eyes were wide at the thought of Daniel's children.

Something flickered in his eyes, the emotion unreadable. 'Don't you want children?'

'It isn't that——'

'You don't want *my* children,' he grated incorrectly. 'Well, resign yourself to the fact that they're the only ones you will have; I'm having no cuckoo in my nest!' His expression was grim.

It was so close a description of what *she* had been that for a moment Heather was silent. Then the thought of children of her own warmed her, Daniel's children. Oh *yes,* she wanted them! 'I'd like to give you children, Daniel,' she told him huskily.

His mouth twisted. 'I'll try to make it an enjoyable experience for you!'

She sat back tiredly. She was constantly fighting a solid wall of contempt, and at this moment she was too exhausted to fight any more.

She released her hand from his as quickly as possible once he had helped her out of the car, sweeping into the hotel slightly ahead of him to wait for their guests to begin arriving from the church. Everything went smoothly until Phillip arrived, his secretary his partner for the day.

Heather hadn't noticed him amongst the other guests at the church, had had eyes only for Daniel, and it was only now that she saw how grim Phillip looked. She glanced at Daniel as the other man approached them, angry at the derision in his expression.

'Phillip,' she greeted warmly to make up for Daniel's lack of enthusiasm, placing both her hands in his. 'How lovely to see you!'

He kissed her, not on the cheek as the other guests had done, but lingeringly on the mouth. 'I wish it could have been in different circumstances,' he countered quietly.

She hadn't meant to encourage him with her warmth, only to show her pleasure that he had come at all! She could feel the displeasure emanating from Daniel.

'Sorry,' Daniel drawled insincerely. 'But I'm the only husband Heather will ever have.'

Phillip gave the other man a dismissive glance before turning back to Heather. 'My offer still stands,' he muttered before grasping his secretary's arm and striding off towards the bar.

'What offer?' Daniel predictably grated at her side once the other man was out of earshot.

She sighed. 'He was only trying to antagonise you—as you were him!'

'What offer, Heather?' he repeated in a controlled voice, that very control dangerous.

She gave another sigh. 'Just that if I ever need a friend, he's available.'

'I'll just bet he is,' muttered Daniel, his arms about her as he nuzzled against her ear, looking for all the world as if he couldn't keep his hands off her. And maybe he couldn't, but from the anger emanating from him Heather had a feeling he would rather his hands were *around her throat!* 'Pull another stunt like that,' he warned harshly, 'and I'll book us into a room right here and make love to you!' He gave a harsh laugh as she trembled. 'And, as you've so rightly guessed, I would be far from gentle!'

Her shiver had been one of anticipation, not fear. But she couldn't allow Daniel to believe he could intimidate her at will. She moved pointedly out of his arms. 'Pull another stunt like *this*,' she told him softly, 'and *you'll* find yourself in more trouble than you can handle.' She stepped back as his eyes widened appreciatively. 'Now, if you could force yourself to be civilised for a short while longer, I believe our guests are waiting for us to begin the dancing.'

His mouth quirked. 'I hope you relax yourself enough in bed to forget for a while that you're supposed to be a lady!'

'Why?' she taunted, arching dark brows. 'Have you never made love to one before?'

His lips thinned. 'Very funny,' he rasped. 'Let's get this dance over with so I can get myself a whisky!'

It was only the second time he had ever danced with her, and this time was worse than the first, Daniel's anger a tangible thing between them, the music seeming to go on for ever.

'Why did you never ask me to dance at any of my father's parties?' Heather asked suddenly, aware of a sea of avidly curious faces watching their every move.

He glanced down at her. 'I rarely dance; surely you've noticed that,' he finally bit out.

'Yes, but——'

'And never with little girls who have a crush on me,' he added harshly.

All the colour drained from Heather's cheeks as she stared at him in horror. 'You——' She began again, her voice gruff. 'You knew?'

He shrugged. 'You weren't exactly subtle. And having some little teenager touch me for the sake of it didn't appeal to me.'

Oh, God, she thought, not just her father had guessed at her feelings for this man, but the man himself had known, too! And she had thought she had hidden her feelings so well. 'I'll always be thirteen years younger than you.'

Daniel shook his head. 'I doubt it will matter when I'm fifty and you're thirty-seven. As for now, you're two years older—and a hell of a lot wiser, I hope!'

But she wasn't as far as loving this man was concerned, for she still loved him. And it devastated her to know that he had realised how she had felt about him two years ago. Although not now, now he seemed in complete ignorance of the fact that what he had assumed was a 'crush' had developed into a deep, abiding love. Maybe that was because he refused to recognise love.

But she knew when he said 'wiser' he didn't mean that he hoped she had more sense than to love him now, he meant she had to be more experienced, knew that love wasn't at all necessary to a relationship. If she felt that way she would be as hardened as he was and, even though it hurt to love him, she knew it would hurt more *not* to love him. Daniel had been alone for so long, hadn't allowed love into his life, but he wasn't alone any longer, and while she wasn't about to let him totally dominate her, surely her love would eventually reach inside him and spark a response. It was all she had to cling on to.

'Am I?' she said lightly, her expression deliberately candid as he looked at her sharply.

'Heather——'

'Don't look so worried, Daniel,' she mocked as he suddenly looked very uncertain. 'I'm not about to bore you with protestations of love.'

'I wouldn't be bored,' he said harshly. 'I would be rather incredulous that you had managed to fall in love with the husband you've had forced upon you!'

He wouldn't be incredulous at all, he would be sceptical and disbelieving! 'That would be a little difficult to accept, wouldn't it?' she agreed drily—because if Daniel hadn't been that man she would have forfeited everything rather than marry a man her father chose for her.

'Impossible,' he nodded curtly, his mouth curled scornfully.

Her eyes glowed deep purple. 'But that doesn't mean we can't take what we can from this marriage,' she invited softly.

'Each other?' he taunted.

'Why not?' she shrugged.

'We'll know after tonight, won't we?' he drawled, stepping away from her as the music came to an end, nodding acknowledgement of their guests' polite clapping at the end of their solo dance together. 'I wonder who will be applauding then?' he mocked before her uncle took his place.

The strain of returning Daniel's barbs, and

giving a few of her own, was beginning to tell
on Heather, and she trembled slightly from the
respite as she stepped gratefully into her uncle's
arms. She wasn't sure how much more of this
she could take!

Her uncle chuckled softly, completely misun-
derstanding the reason for her strained
appearance. 'I should have told the two of you
to go off and get married quietly somewhere;
it's less of a strain on the emotions—and the
nerves!'

She had thought Daniel would prefer a quiet
wedding, had suggested as much to him, only
to have him come back with the comment—she
didn't want all her snobby friends to witness
her marriage to one of the lower classes! After
that, nothing would have deterred her from
having the biggest and grandest wedding she
could organise in so short a time, the guest list
numbering in the five hundreds, and none of
them Daniel's relatives or friends. When she
had asked him for his guest list he had told her
he didn't have any family he would want to
invite, and he very much doubted she would
welcome the 'friend' he could have invited!
Guessing who that 'friend' was, Heather hadn't
pressed him any more.

'Never mind,' her uncle sympathised. 'The
two of you can make your escape soon.'

'There's no rush.' Her bravado with Daniel
had been exactly that, her fear of the wedding
night as strong now as it had been in the church
earlier, so that she had missed most of the

marriage service. Stronger, because she was now frightened that, once in Daniel's arms, she might unconsciously reveal the love she felt for a man who could only view the emotion with contempt. 'We aren't going anywhere but home, so why shouldn't we enjoy our own wedding reception?'

'True,' her uncle nodded. 'And it isn't as if you can't wait to be alone together.'

Uncle Lionel believed this would be a marriage of pure convenience, she could read that unspoken statement in what he had said! 'I—we were discussing children earlier.' Her voice was husky as she told him in the only way she could, without embarrassing them both, that it wasn't going to be that way. 'Daniel would like several.'

'Heather——'

'It's all right, Uncle Lionel,' she soothed his distressed protest. 'I really would like that, too. So if Stella asks again,' she added lightly, 'you can tell her that Daniel and I *will* be sharing a bed.'

'She's only concerned for you, as I am,' he defended, frowning. 'Even more so now. Heather, it isn't too late to have the marriage annulled.'

They said love was blind, and where Stella was concerned it certainly made Uncle Lionel so; Stella had never been concerned for anyone else but herself in the whole of her life! 'I don't want the marriage annulled,' she assured him.

'Daniel is a hard man——'

'He's only what his life so far has made him,'

she defended. 'I could so easily have turned out the same way.'

'Is that why you——?'

'No,' she cut in quickly. 'You know why I married him.' Not even to her beloved uncle could she admit her love for Daniel.

'Is the airline worth a lifetime of misery?' he frowned. 'The way Max's will is worded only death could give either of you full control of AI now.'

Heather shivered, glancing quickly across the room to where Daniel was dancing with Stella. She would want to die, too, if anything ever happened to him!

As if sensing her gaze on him he raised his head and turned to look at her, frowning at how pale she was. Afraid that her love—a love he rejected without knowing of its existence —might be revealed in her eyes, she quickly turned away. 'Our marriage will work,' she vowed vehemently to her uncle. 'You'll see.'

'I hope so,' he returned without conviction.

It was a glittering social evening, the number of guests meaning that the bride and groom were rarely together, and never alone. But, as midnight neared, Daniel invited her to dance again. Heather went willingly into his arms, the champagne she had drunk most of the evening relaxing her.

'Unless you want a scene I think you'd better deal with that situation,' Daniel rasped as soon as they were on the dance-floor.

Heather blinked up into his disapproving face.

'I've only had a few glasses of champagne——'

'*You* can drink yourself unconscious for all I care,' he interrupted harshly. 'I'm talking about *him!*'

She followed his gaze to the bar, suddenly completely sober as she saw Phillip hadn't moved from the spot he had taken up as soon as he arrived. Penny, his secretary, was obviously trying to persuade him to leave, while he was intent on seeing the bottom of the bottle of whisky he had ordered to be left beside him.

'Quite,' Daniel bit out impatiently as Heather's stricken gaze returned to him. 'You must be good if the thought of you spending the night in another man's arms reduces Wingate to *that!*'

Even now, when their marriage was a fact, he couldn't stop insulting her! 'Why don't you sort that little problem out and we'll go home and find out——?'

He grasped her arm as she would have turned away. 'From the look of Wingate it's far from a "little" problem, and it certainly isn't mine! You should have made the position clear to Wingate weeks ago,' he added grimly.

Her eyes flashed. 'As you did with Cassandra?'

'Yes!'

'Maybe I don't have as much experience at hurting people as you do,' she scorned.

Daniel's eyes were steely slits. 'Get over there and tell Wingate he'd better leave here quietly or he's out of a job. And then meet me outside; maybe it *is* time I found out how good you are!'

CHAPTER FIVE

HEATHER burned with resentment as Daniel strode across the room to talk to her uncle, sparing valuable seconds to glare after her husband before going determinedly towards Phillip.

He seemed to blanch as he saw the fury in her eyes. 'Heather, I——'

'Daniel believes it's time you left,' she declared fiercely, all her sympathy for this man gone when it put her at the mercy of Daniel's cutting tongue. 'And so do I!' she added as Phillip seemed about to argue.

'You know why I——'

'It doesn't matter *why* you're choosing to make an idiot of yourself,' she cut in angrily. 'You *are* doing it, and it has to stop. Let Penny take you home.'

'But I——'

'Do it, Wingate,' a harsh voice instructed coldly. 'Or start looking for another job first thing Monday morning.'

After the way he had spoken to her minutes earlier, Daniel was the last person Heather had expected to help her, although she admitted she needed help; Penny seemed as much at a loss as to how to deal with Phillip as she was, looking very distressed.

Phillip put down his empty glass. 'You don't deserve her, Taggart,' he ground out.

'But I've got her—' Grey eyes were flinty, '—and what's mine I keep!'

'Until you tire of it, or it outlives its usefulness.' Phillip threw all caution to the winds. 'And when you tire of Heather *I'll* be around to pick up the pieces!'

'You like other men's leftovers, do you?' taunted Daniel, voice dangerously soft.

Phillip's face was flushed. 'You aren't good enough to be in the same room as Heather.'

'I'm good enough to pay your wages,' Daniel returned icily. 'Although I'm dangerously close to reconsidering that!'

Phillip's mouth twisted into a sneer. 'Go ahead, fire me. With my qualifications I can get a job anywhere.'

'Phillip——'

Daniel grasped hold of Heather's arm, painfully cutting off her protest. 'Why don't you think about doing that? And soon!'

'Come on, Penny,' Phillip scorned. 'Our host thinks we've outstayed our welcome.'

'Not Penny, just you, Wingate,' Daniel corrected gratingly.

Penny threw him a grateful look for his assurances before helping Phillip from the room, the latter slightly unsteady on his feet.

Heather was shaken from the encounter, leaning weakly into Daniel as his arm came supportively about her waist.

'You really will have to learn how to tell a man "no" convincingly,' he softly derided.

She stiffened, regretting lowering her guard with him in even a moment's weakness. 'Maybe I should practise on you,' she snapped, moving away from him.

He looked amused by the challenge. 'From the way you've behaved with me so far, I would say you might find that a little difficult to do!' He arched mocking brows.

Heather paled at the taunt. 'There are hundreds—thousands!—of men with as much experience—more!—than you have!'

He gave a mocking inclination of his head. 'And after the next two months have elapsed no doubt you'll feel free to get to know every single one of them personally!'

Why did she love this man? Was it really *possible* to love someone who was incapable of feeling love himself? Why was she torturing herself with these questions? she silently admonished herself; she couldn't *talk* herself out of loving him!

'Is Cassandra willing to wait the two months for you?' She attacked rather than defended.

Daniel instantly looked bored. 'Cassandra's—charms had already begun to pall; our marriage was as good a reason as any to end things.'

'Do you usually need a reason?' Heather scorned.

'No,' he admitted abruptly. 'I've never seen

any necessity to pretend an interest I no longer feel.'

'I'm sure the woman involved gets the customary trinket at the end of the affair,' she derided.

Daniel's expression darkened. 'The only woman I've ever offered jewellery to is you, and you turned down an engagement ring. If a woman wants to enjoy a relationship with me then that's fine by me, but I've never asked any woman to whore herself for me!'

Heather frowned at his vehemence in return to her mild barb. 'I didn't mean——'

'If you want to know more about women who sell themselves, ask me about my mother some time,' he cut in glacially. 'But not now!'

Heather felt a physical ache in her chest for the pain his words uncovered. He had told her he had never known his father, had claimed his mother was stupid and naïve, and now he had revealed that it had been these two things that made him sceptical of love and marriage. It didn't matter that his mother had cared enough to bring him into the world and love him, what she was had been unmistakable to someone as astute as Daniel.

'I told you before, don't pity me!' he rasped as he saw the compassion in her eyes. 'It wasn't such a bad life; until my stepfather came along I had plenty of "uncles" to buy me presents!'

This time she kept her compassion hidden, although it wasn't easy. If only Daniel knew it, they had so much to give each other, had both known only a mother's love, both needed to give the excess of love that had built up inside them over the years to someone, and it should be to each other.

'What's the matter, little rich girl?' he suddenly taunted. 'The son of a woman who slept around so that she could support us not good enough to be your husband?'

The pain, oh, God! the pain their mothers had both subjected them to, whether willingly or not. 'Is your mother still alive?' she asked.

He shook his head. 'She died a couple of years ago.'

'I'm sorry.'

Daniel's eyes narrowed. 'Why, would she have been guest of honour at our wedding?' he scorned.

After Heather's conception the only man in her mother's life had been Max Danvers, but was she any less guilty of selling herself, and her child, than Daniel's mother had been? Heather didn't think so. 'I would have liked to have met her,' she said softly.

'I don't think so,' he muttered. 'Heather Danvers and Julia Taggart would have had little in common!'

'My name is Taggart too now,' she reminded him quietly, not upset by his derision, understanding more than he knew his need to hit out. How many times had she inwardly stormed at her mother for marrying Max Danvers!

'It isn't a name to be proud of,' he snapped.

'The stepfather who gave it to me was a lazy drunkard!'

She put a hand on Daniel's arm. 'I'm very proud to call myself your wife,' she told him huskily.

'I'm sure,' he drawled in an amused voice. 'Let's get out of here and make it fact rather than just a title.'

Heather was filled with a quiet calm at his effort to shock her once again, she knew so much more about this man, understood him so much better than she had this morning. He didn't want love but he needed it, and she was going to give it to him.

Their goodbyes were made laughingly, Daniel easily returning some of the more personal comments that were being made, and the only moment of awkwardness was introduced by Stella.

'I saw poor Phillip being led out of here drunk,' she snapped accusingly. 'The poor man is devastated.'

Daniel's mouth twisted as Heather gasped. 'Why don't you go and offer to console him, Stella?' he drawled.

Blue eyes flashed with fury. 'Maybe I will,' Stella finally challenged, glancing at her husband across the room from them. 'Someone should show him that *she* isn't worth ruining his life over.' She glared at Heather.

'And I'm sure you're the woman to do it,' Daniel mocked.

'Why you——'

'We really do have to go now,' Heather cut in firmly. 'Interesting as this conversation is.' And it *was* interesting, more so than she had at first realised. She knew Stella better than to believe her only concern was Phillip, knew that anything the other woman did or said had a selfish reasoning behind it. Stella had mentioned Phillip to antagonise, and from the way she kept reminding Daniel of Heather's past relationship with the other man, she didn't think it was *her* the other woman was trying to antagonise.

She glanced at Daniel as he sat behind the wheel of his car, the vehicle having been delivered to the hotel during the course of the evening. Not that any of the guests had realised that, so they had been spared the traditional trappings that would otherwise have been attached to the car.

'Ask, Heather,' Daniel rasped in the darkness after they had been driving for several minutes.

She gave a start. 'What——?'

'You've been longing to know if there was ever anything between Stella and me ever since the thought occurred to you the day we stepped out of the lift together at Air International,' he bit out coldly.

Heather moistened her lips, knowing it was true. And she was *sure* Stella hadn't been baiting her minutes ago. 'Well, was there? Or is there?' she added breathlessly, not sure she really wanted to hear the answer.

'No.'

Just that, no explanations or assurances, just flat denial. And because she believed she knew Daniel, she believed *him*. 'I'm glad.' She sighed her relief. 'For Uncle Lionel's sake,' she added hastily.

'How can you be sure I'm not lying to you?' Daniel demanded.

She shrugged, relaxing back in her seat. 'Because I doubt you would lie to save me the humiliation of knowing you bedded my aunt!'

'Why should knowing about Stella—who, by the way, does nothing for me—differ from knowing about Cassandra?' he frowned.

She shook her head. 'It just does.'

Daniel gave an impatient sigh. 'Maybe it would be best if we avoided discussing past relationships.'

'That's fine with me,' she accepted gladly, feeling pain every time she thought of the other women who had been in his life.

'I thought it might be,' he drawled. 'What's the matter, scared I might want to know how many other executives at Air International you've slept with?'

The flush to her cheeks was pure anger. 'Let's hope you find the experience I've gained from all these lovers worth it!'

'It's what I've waited a month to find out!' he mocked.

The silence between them for the rest of the journey was far from companionable. Heather was brooding about how she was supposed to act experienced when she knew nothing about lovemaking except what she had read in romantic books, and Daniel's thoughts were as private as the rest of him. They were still silent as they let themselves into the house and went through to the lounge.

'How thoughtful,' drawled Daniel when he saw the plate of covered sandwiches and the pot of coffee left out for them on the table.

Heather ignored his derision, pouring them both a cup of coffee, her stomach churning at the sight of the sandwiches.

Daniel watched her with cold eyes, ignoring his own coffee. 'I need a shower.' He pulled off his tie and unbuttoned his shirt at the throat. 'Care to show me which room is ours?'

She swallowed with difficulty. 'It's the one I've always used——'

'Only a single bed?' He arched his dark brows. 'My, we are going to be cosy, aren't we?'

'Why do you have to be so difficult?' Her eyes flashed her anger. 'Do you think any of this has been easy for me? Do you think I wanted to marry you this way?' She was breathing hard in her agitation.

His eyes were narrowed to icy slits. 'I think you wanted your inheritance any way you could get it!'

'I didn't have to agree to sleep with you, too!'

'No,' he acknowledged slowly. 'Are you curious to know what it would be like to make love with the savage, too? Stella has a voice that carries,' he derided as her eyes widened.

And 'savage' was one of the more polite

things Stella had called him at their engagement party! 'I'm sorry you had to hear that.'

'I'm not,' he scorned. 'You didn't answer my question.'

Heather wasn't curious about making love with him, she was terrified! He scorned everything, every soft emotion there was, and she dreaded his ridicule if he should ever guess at her innocence.

Her head went back challengingly. 'I've been looking forward to it!'

Daniel gave a mocking inclination of his head. 'Then let's take a shower and put you out of your misery.'

She was glad she had given the staff the night off, she couldn't have borne for them to witness the antagonism Daniel displayed towards her.

She met his mocking gaze as he turned from looking at the double bed she had had moved into her room to replace the single bed she had used in the past; the only other double bed in the house had been the one in the room her parents had shared, and she refused to share that one with Daniel.

'Pity,' he derided. 'I've never tried to share a single bed.'

The colour seemed to be a permanent light in her cheeks. 'There are other rooms if you would rather——'

'I wouldn't.' He was suddenly standing very close. 'This will do just fine.' His lips trailed down her cheek to her throat.

Heather jerked away as if he had burnt her.

'You use the bathroom first.' She turned away. 'I—I'll just clear away in the lounge.'

'I'm sure it isn't expected of you,' he drawled.

'I'd like to do it,' she insisted sharply.

Daniel watched her go with a mocking grin curving his lips as he slowly unbuttoned his shirt down his chest.

Her hands shook badly as she carried the untouched sandwiches and the pot of coffee through to the kitchen, needing something to do to fill the minutes until she and Daniel shared a bed for the first time.

It was all so much worse than she had expected! How could she act the sophisticate when no man had ever seen her naked, ever caressed her body until she cried out for satisfaction? What was she supposed to *do,* for goodness' sake?

'Are you going to day-dream in here all night?'

She turned so suddenly at the sound of Daniel's voice that she almost knocked a cup off the tray at the sight of him, his hair damp, his chest bare, a towel draped about his hips. At least he had spared her the embarrassment of seeing him walking around naked!

'I—er—I wasn't sure how long you would be,' she excused herself, unable to look at him after that first glance.

He shrugged. 'I'm not averse to a little company while I shave. Or when I shower either, for that matter,' he smiled.

Without one of the formal suits he favoured,

and with his hair still damp he looked more approachable, and Heather was able to envisage the lean length of his body beneath the covering towel. Just the thought of it made her tremble.

'I won't be long.' She brushed past him and hurried to the bathroom without a backward glance.

She leant weakly against the wall, the bathroom still hot from the heat of the water Daniel had run minutes earlier, a razor, aftershave, and a toothbrush in the cabinet beside her own. Daniel's suitcases had been delivered this morning, and she had no doubt that, if she looked in the closets and drawers, Daniel's clothes would be neatly beside hers, too.

She deliberately made her mind a blank as she went through her nightly toilet, lingering over the brushing of her hair with leisurely strokes, pleased to have it loose about her shoulders once again. It was only as she turned to leave the bathroom that she realised she hadn't brought a nightgown in here with her!

For a moment she panicked, envisaged staying in here all night because she was too embarrassed to ask Daniel to pass her a nightgown. But she realised he would never let her get away with that, and if she walked out of here naked surely that would enhance the impression of sophistication; she would look far too much like a virginal bride in a nightgown!

The lights had been blazing in the bedroom as she passed through it to take her shower, but now only the bedside lamp illuminated the room, and although nothing could hide her nakedness from his gaze, at least the dimmed lighting threw her body into shadow. Not that she had anything to be ashamed of, her breasts firm and uptilting, tipped by dusky rose, her waist slender, her hips silky soft, her legs long and shapely.

'Heather, I—my God . . . !'

She drew in a deep steadying breath as she raised her gaze to look at Daniel. He lay in the middle of the bed, both pillows behind his shoulders as he leant back against the head-board, his chest golden in the lamplight, covered in the wiry dark hair sprinkled with grey.

Heather didn't hesitate, knowing that if she did she would turn around and run from the room. Instead of that she walked steadily to the side of the bed, pulled back the bedclothes, and slowly lay down on top of Daniel, her mouth lowering to claim his.

'What the he-hell . . . !' He groaned as her lips claimed his and her body moved erotically against him.

She had never taken the initiative with any man before, and because Daniel hadn't been expecting her to do so now she caught him completely off guard, his thighs a velvet throb as they surged hard against her. He *did* respond to her!

Filled with a sense of powerful exhilaration, she increased the pressure of her mouth on his, their mouths parting as she ran the tip of her tongue along his lower lip, tasting the mint of his toothpaste, the smell of his elusive spicy aftershave filling her senses.

Her breasts nestled against the wiry hair on his chest, the tips hard and aching from the rough caress, a warm ache between her thighs as she felt Daniel instinctively probing there. Far from not knowing what to do with a naked man in a bed, she now knew exactly what she wanted, longing to be filled by Daniel, to know the powerful surge of him inside her as he satisfied that ache!

'What the hell do you think you're doing?' Daniel rasped harshly as she moved her hips against him.

Heather blinked down at him bewilderedly, having been completely enthralled by the sensual pleasure she had known as soon as her body touched his. And she had thought he felt the pleasure too, the way he throbbed against her had said that he did.

He looked at her coldly. 'I can't stand aggressive women, in—or out of—bed!' he rasped, leaving her in no doubt that was what he considered her.

CHAPTER SIX

HEATHER moved abruptly away from him as she realised exactly what she had done. She had tried to be the experienced woman she had thought he expected, and instead he had made her feel cheap and demanding. She hadn't seemed experienced at all to him, just man-hungry! How could they go on after this?

She closed her eyes, clutching the sheet over a body that now felt cold, icily cold. 'I'm sorry,' she finally groaned.

Daniel moved impatiently beside her. 'What did you think you were doing?' he demanded again.

Her eyes were still squeezed tightly shut. 'I said I was sorry,' she choked.

'Surely you weren't *that* hungry for a man that you thought you actually wanted *me*?' he scorned.

Her lids flew wide. Of course she had wanted him, more than that—at that moment she had loved him more than ever before. 'We *are* married——'

'So we are,' he sighed disgustedly. 'And you find the idea of sex with your husband more exciting than all those lovers, do you?'

'I——'

'I always thought taking a lover was supposed to be more erotic,' he said harshly, his eyes steely. 'Unless, of course, you were pretending I was someone else?' His eyes narrowed.

'Of course not,' she instantly protested, her cheeks flaming. 'If I went about this all wrong, then I'm sorry, but——'

'All wrong?' Daniel repeated incredulously, throwing back the bedclothes to get out of the bed, unconcerned with his nakedness. 'I'm sure every bridegroom wishes he had a bride as *eager* as you were just now!'

Heather wanted to die or, if she was to be spared that final act, to at least crawl into a hiding-place until this whole humiliating experience was over! But fate was never that kind, and painful as this was, she had to live through it. And as she had already learnt, with this man attack was the best form of defence.

'What did you expect, Daniel?' she challenged. 'A little virgin bride cringing beneath the covers as she waited to be claimed sacrificially by her husband?' Her eyes flashed, magnificently purple in that moment.

'That would have been too much to hope for, in the circumstances,' he drawled insultingly. 'However, a little reticence on your part might have been nice. It might have at least given the impression of ladylike modesty! Only Heather Danvers is no lady, is she?' he scoffed.

'Just because all you've ever had in your life is——Oh, my God, Daniel, I wasn't going to say that,' she choked as his face paled dramatically, his eyes dark pools of anger. 'Never that! Daniel——'

'Get away from me!' He threw off her hand as she reached for him. 'Give a woman a little ammunition and she'll throw it at you the first time things don't go completely her way! Only what my mother was during her life no longer matters to me,' he snapped furiously. 'What I've *married* does!' He glared at her with dislike. 'Our deal to try and make this marriage work is off, Heather; I couldn't even force myself to take you now!'

She moved up on her knees as he turned to leave. 'You'll never have the chance again!' She angrily vented her fury on him—or she would have broken down and cried.

He paused only long enough to get some clothes out of the cupboards and drawers, turning to look at her coldly. 'Don't kid yourself, Heather,' he scorned confidently. 'I could take you any time I wanted to.' The door closed quietly behind him.

He was right—oh God, how right he was! She would never be able to say no to him.

She had ruined it all, had repulsed Daniel with her eagerness. She doubted he would ever *want* to make love to her again.

Her eyes were heavy with tiredness as she made her way downstairs the next morning.

She had no idea where Daniel had spent the

night, and the maid hadn't volunteered the information of his whereabouts when she had brought in the tray of coffee to her earlier. The other woman certainly hadn't seemed surprised *not* to find Daniel in the bed with her. It was more than Heather's pride could stand for her to *ask* where her husband was.

The breakfast trays were still set out in the dining-room, but Heather bypassed that room, just the smell of the food making her feel ill.

If only she hadn't hit out with that purely defensive remark about the other women in Daniel's life, a remark he had taken as a personal slur on his mother, maybe they could have worked things out. Now it was too late. Daniel could even have moved out already for all she knew. There was nothing in her father's will to say they actually had to live together.

'Would you like breakfast served in here this morning, Miss—Mrs Taggart?' the butler self-consciously corrected himself.

Heather turned from gazing sightlessly out of one of the tall lounge windows. 'I'm really not hungry, thank you, Shilton.' She gave a wan smile. 'If—Mr Taggart has eaten you might as well clear away,' she added, tensing for his answer.

The elderly man frowned. 'I don't believe Mr Taggart had time for breakfast this morning. I do hope he won't be gone too long,' he added sympathetically.

Oh God, Daniel hadn't even spared her this humiliation, he had left the house as soon as

he was able. How long would it be before
everyone knew that he hadn't even spent one
night in her bed with her before returning to
his bachelor existence? He hadn't given her, or
this marriage, a chance, and now he never
would.

'Let's hope so,' she replied non-committally.
'Could you have my car brought round? I—I
think I'll go out for a while.'

She didn't know where she was going, hadn't
given it any thought, she just knew she had to
get away from the house and the memories
her bedroom evoked. Would she ever forget
the humiliation she had suffered there?

She sat outside the new house for a long
time trying to decide whether or not she should
go in. Big, with five bedrooms up the wide
staircase, it still in no way matched the size of
her father's house. It was the house she and
Daniel had chosen for their own.

After the episode with the engagement ring
she hadn't expected any help from Daniel in
choosing their new home, and had looked at
several houses in London before being shown
this one just out of town. It was a beautiful
Georgian-style house, with an apartment over
the garage that would be ideal for Shilton and
his wife Edna, who also happened to be their
cook. Heather had decided that any other staff
they had could come in on a casual basis.
Fired by her enthusiastic description of the
house, Daniel had asked to see it. She had
fallen in love with the house on sight, and had

felt nervous about Daniel's agreement when it was so far out of town. He hadn't seemed particularly impressed, but he hadn't turned it down either, and the sale had gone ahead. Now it didn't seem worth moving into if Daniel weren't going to be there with her.

The carpet had been put down in the lounge—a deep, smoky grey that reminded her of the colour of Daniel's eyes—since she had last been here. All the finishing touches, such as carpets and curtains, had still to be completed, and yet, as she looked around at the quiet elegance, Heather knew she and Daniel could have been happy here. Or as happy as they could have been together anywhere.

Not for the first time, she wondered why her father had done this to them. She knew he hated her, but he had come to love her mother; how could he have wanted to destroy his wife's child in this way? The answer to that was all too obvious; she hadn't been *his* child.

What would she and Daniel do with this house now? She had chosen all the furniture and fittings with Daniel's comfort in mind, and there would be even more to haunt her here if she chose to live here alone once her father's house was gone.

There was no word from Daniel when she got back to the house, and it was only when Shilton asked if they could prepare her a late supper that she realised she hadn't eaten since the wedding reception. Just thinking of that robbed her of any appetite she may have had. She had only been married a day and already her marriage was in tatters.

Daniel's clothes remained next to hers in the wardrobes and drawers, and she wondered if she should pack them up for him. But she had nowhere she could send them to other than his office, and she doubted he would thank her if she sent them there. No doubt he would let her know what he wanted done with them soon enough.

When he staggered into the house later that evening, looking totally exhausted, the stubble dark on his chin, his clothes creased, Heather had the shock of her life.

Unwilling to go to the bed she had so briefly shared with Daniel, she had chosen to sit in the lounge instead, the book she had brought with her still open on the first page. She had felt as if she were in a long, dark tunnel that had no end. But the beginning had assuredly been last night.

It had taken her several seconds to realise the front door had opened and closed, several more motionless seconds to realise Shilton couldn't have opened the door because she had told him over an hour ago that he wouldn't be needed any more tonight. The realisation that it must be Daniel returning came very quickly after that, and with it a trembling nervousness.

She had half risen from her chair by the time he entered the room, her eyes widening as she took in his appearance.

He walked straight past her to the array of
drinks in the cabinet behind her, swallowing
down half a glass of fiery brandy before turning
to acknowledge her presence. 'Don't tell me
my little wife has waited up for me,' he
drawled, drinking the rest of the brandy. 'How
nice!'

She was used to his insults by now, and it
was the fact that he was obviously still wearing—and had been for some time, by their
creased appearance—the clothes he had pulled
so haphazardly from the wardrobe and drawers
the previous night that caused her to continue
staring at him. Could he have been as disturbed
by last night as she was?

'I must say,' he drawled softly, 'I expected
you to be a little more vocal than this!'

Colour darkened her pale cheeks. 'I don't
know what to say,' she shrugged—and she
didn't! Not without angering him again
anyway. Where had he been? *Who* had he been
with?

His mouth twisted. 'You could start with,
"Is it all over?", "Are——?" '

'Is it?' She swallowed hard.

'Obviously,' he drawled, 'or I wouldn't be
here now.'

She frowned. 'But——'

'Can we leave the questioning until
tomorrow, Heather?' he rasped, his expression
grim. 'It's been one hell of a day, and I'm
damned tired.'

She was more confused than ever. If their marriage was over, as he had just said it was, what was he doing here? It was obvious he intended staying, for he began unbuttoning his shirt as he strode out of the room.

Heather almost had to run to keep up with him as he went towards their bedroom. 'Daniel, what——?'

'Is there anything to eat in the kitchen?' he frowned, throwing off his shirt. 'Or do you only know how to eat food and not how to cook it?'

She came to an abrupt halt in the middle of the bedroom that had seemed like a place of torture since he left it so abruptly the night before. 'I'll gladly get you something to eat,' she told him in a controlled voice, 'if you'll just tell me what's going on!'

Unabashed by her presence, Daniel removed his trousers, and his brief black underpants quickly followed his shirt on to the chair. 'There was no bomb, not here in London, not in Manchester, not in any of the planes. I know, because I was with the police when they searched every damned one of them,' he added grimly. 'Now, if you don't mind, I need a shower.'

Heather stared at him as if she had never seen him before. 'You mean, they thought there was a bomb in one of our buildings?' She clutched at his arm.

Grey eyes narrowed. 'Don't tell me you didn't know——'

'But I didn't,' she gasped, very pale. 'How could I?'

'You haven't seen the television, listened to the radio?' Daniel frowned his disbelief.

'No, I—I haven't felt like doing anything since—since you left,' she admitted reluctantly. 'And all the staff have been tiptoeing around me all day; I thought it was because they pitied me, because my husband of one day had walked out on me.' Her eyes were wide. 'Daniel, what happened?' she squeaked.

He scowled. 'We received a call that there was a bomb on Air International property. No other details, just that.'

'I had no idea . . . ' Heather was shaking badly. While she had been mooning about feeling sorry for herself . . . ! 'There was no bomb, you said?' She blinked, the enormity of the situation sweeping over her.

'Can all this wait, Heather?' he snapped impatiently. 'I've been running around like a madman all day, and I'm tired and hungry.'

There were so many things she still wanted to know, so many questions to ask, and yet she knew that when Daniel was feeling so weary and in need of food it wasn't the time. 'Give me fifteen minutes and I'll have a meal waiting for you in the kitchen.'

But only half-way through that fifteen minutes some of her concern had turned to anger, and by the time the steaming hot meal of steak and baked potato was on the break-fast-bar waiting for Daniel, she was absolutely furious. She was a partner in Air International, she should have been informed along with Daniel of the bomb threat, should have been at his side during the ordeal. Instead of which he was treating her like a clinging wife who was being too curious about things that didn't concern her!

The mildness of her expression told him nothing of her mood when he joined her a few minutes later, as she served him a salad to go with his steak and potato, then sat down beside him, although her own meal remained untouched. She had mistakenly thought, when she began cooking, that with Daniel's return she had found her own appetite. She was too angry to eat!

'I owe you an apology,' Daniel drawled after finishing his first tender mouthful of the steak.

'Oh?' she prompted stiffly. He owed her more than an apology, damn him!

He nodded. 'You *can* cook,' he taunted. 'This steak is delicious.'

Heather drew in a ragged breath. 'I'm so glad it meets with your approval,' she returned with saccharine sweetness.

'It does,' he declared, taking another healthy mouthful, of potato this time, obviously savouring its fluffy perfection.

'Tell me,' she prompted, her voice deceptively soft, 'did my uncle know about this bomb scare?'

'Of course,' Daniel dismissed impatiently. 'I informed him as soon as the police had contacted me. You aren't eating.' He suddenly seemed to realise the food on her plate had remained untouched.

'I've decided I'm not hungry, after all,' she answered coldly. 'Did the senior executives at Air International know about it, too?'

'They were notified just in case we found anything,' he nodded. 'We had a little trouble locating Wingate, by the way,' he added tauntingly. 'But I finally remembered how softhearted Penny is, and the fact that Wingate was completely stoned when he left last night. He was sleeping on Penny's sofa, where she could keep an eye on him,' Daniel derided. 'Do you mind if I . . . ?' His fork hovered over her rapidly cooling steak. 'As you aren't hungry.'

'No, take it,' she said impatiently. 'And just for the record, Phillip could have been asleep on *Penny* for all his whereabouts last night concern me!'

'Naughty, naughty,' Daniel taunted. 'I don't think he was capable of being with any woman in that way last night. Well . . . perhaps one woman I can think of!' He smiled at the private memory.

'He could have had a dozen women in his bed and it wouldn't have bothered me.' She angrily clarified the fact that she didn't care where—or with whom—Phillip slept.

'It might have bothered them,' Daniel mocked. 'Do we have any wine to go with this?' He was looking much more refreshed after partially eating the meal.

As several bottles stood at room temperature in the wine rack across the kitchen he had to know they did!

Heather's movements were quick and economical as she opened the bottle and poured some of the ruby-red wine into a glass for him.

He sipped it appreciatively, his eyes mocking over the glass rim. 'Something else they taught you at your expensive finishing school?' he taunted. 'Just in case the man is incapacitated and you need a drink desperately?'

Her mouth tightened. 'Something like that,' she bit out. 'When did you receive the call about the bomb scare, Daniel?' she persisted.

He gave it some thought. 'I was sitting in the lounge going over some papers—you might remember it was a little too hot in bed last night?' he challenged softly.

Her cheeks burnt. 'It cooled very quickly,' she muttered, eyes narrowed.

'Hm,' he derided. 'It must have been about two o'clock when I received the call. Apparently, the police thought it might have been a hoax, but they have to check these things out none the less. I was more than willing to let them!'

'So you took the call here?' she encouraged softly.

'I told you——'

'That's the trouble, Daniel,' she interrupted furiously. 'You didn't tell *me* anything!'

The amusement at her expense faded from his eyes. 'You were asleep——'

'I wasn't! How could I be expected to *sleep* when my husband walked out on me in that way?' Her eyes flashed.

'Now, look——'

'No, *you* look, Daniel,' snapped Heather, glaring at him. 'You told my uncle, your senior executives, the media were obviously informed, and the staff here obviously knew about it too, but you didn't think to tell me, your *partner.*' She was breathing hard in her agitation. 'I had a right to know what was going on!'

'There was nothing you could have done——'

'I had a right to know!' Her voice rose with her anger.

'Why?' His eyes were glacial. 'Because you have your name on a piece of paper that says you own half of *my* airline?' His eyes blazed, his knife and fork were clenched tightly in his hands. 'It takes a damn sight more than that to make you *my* partner.'

'It was my father's airline——'

'It's *mine*,' Daniel rasped harshly. 'I worked twenty hours a day, seven days a week to get that airline back on its feet, and no spoilt little brat with her name on a piece of paper is going to take it away from me!'

He was furiously angry, but her fury matched his. 'I'm your partner, damn it, whether you like it or not, and you'll treat me as such!'

'Will I?'

'Yes!'

Daniel went suddenly still, gently placing his knife and fork down on the almost empty plate in front of him. 'Are you threatening me?'

Heather made an effort to still the trembling his quiet fury evoked. 'If that's what it takes, yes.' She held her head high.

His brows arched as he looked her over very carefully in her black corduroys and loose white blouse, his gaze not missing the trembling of her hands, she felt sure. 'You know something?' he suddenly said softly. 'I don't think this is about today at all.'

'Of course it——'

'No,' he cut in sharply. 'For the last six months you've been perfectly happy to let me deal with any and every problem we've had at AI.' His eyes were narrowed.

'This wasn't just a *problem*——'

'You know what I think *your* problem is?' he challenged softly.

'I'm sure you're about to tell me,' Heather snapped, also sure she wasn't going to like what he said. 'You—Daniel, what do you think you're doing?' she gasped as his hand moved to clasp her arm.

'*Your* problem,' he grated as if she hadn't spoken, 'is that you're furious with me because of last night.' He stood up, walking out of the kitchen, pulling her along behind him.

Her anger faded, to be replaced by apprehension. 'Daniel, what do you think you're doing?' she demanded again.

'I would have thought it was obvious,' he drawled drily.

'Stop this!' she ordered shakily as he tugged her into the bedroom and firmly closed the door behind them.

'Oh no, my little shrew of a wife.' He deftly began to unbutton her blouse. 'I'm going to finish what we started last night—and maybe then you'll stop yelling at me like a fishwife!'

CHAPTER SEVEN

HEATHER trembled at the unmistakable intent in Daniel's set expression.

'Frustration can be hell, can't it?' he mocked as he threw off her blouse and started on her camisole.

This couldn't be happening to her. He couldn't mean to make love to her *now!* But no, she realised as she saw the coldness of his eyes, he didn't intend to *make love* with her at all, just to satisfy a physical need that was as strong for him now as it had been for her last night.

'Daniel, you can't!' she cried, pushing ineffectually at his hands.

'I've changed my mind about that.' He misunderstood the reason for her protest. 'After the day I've just had, a couple of hours' oblivion in your eager arms is *exactly* what I need!'

He was looking at her as if she were some beautiful object he intended lavishing his attention on for a while! 'Daniel, I'm not eager——'

'Of course you are,' he contradicted distractedly, smoothing the camisole down her arms, his gaze feasting on her bared breasts.

'Daniel, I——Ooh!' She gave an aching gasp as his thumb-tip grazed her thrusting nipples. 'Daniel, please——' She broke off and involuntarily her hands moved up, her fingers clasping his hair as she held him against her, her back arched invitingly.

At last he raised his head, her nipple pouting moistly. 'You were saying?' he prompted raggedly.

The respite from the fiery heat of his mouth gave her the strength to tell him the truth she had been afraid to reveal last night. 'Daniel, please don't hurt me,' she pleaded. 'I'm a virgin——'

'Don't take me for a fool, Heather,' he scorned savagely. 'Play the innocent if that's what you want to do, but don't lie to me.'

She swallowed hard. 'It's the truth.'

'Of course it is,' he derided, stripping off her remaining clothes. 'It's an act I'll certainly enjoy more than I did almost being raped last night.' He looked grim. 'Tonight we'll do whatever it takes,' he promised.

His savagery was barely restrained by the forced gentleness of the 'game' but, in the circumstances, Heather knew she couldn't ask for more after the way she had been behaving lately. It was because of that deception, and the pain it had caused her, that she had known she couldn't go on lying to him any more. It was enough, for her, that she had told him the truth at last, that he chose to disbelieve her was his privilege.

His naked body was as magnificent as she remembered it, his chest crushing the sensitivity of her breasts as his mouth claimed hers, the pressure of his lips easing a little as she whimpered her torment.

His hands caressed her hips as he held her against him, moving against her, moaning his pleasure at the contact, his tongue probing her lips to dip into her mouth in the same erotic rhythm.

Her nails dug into his back as the warm sensation washed over her, feeling the moistness between her thighs, instantly wanting him.

If this quicksilver reaction to him made her a wanton, then a wanton she must be, because she felt weak with wanting him!

'Sweet, so damned sweet,' Daniel groaned. 'You taste of honey. And I've always been addicted to honey,' he moaned, before going back for more of the delectable nectar.

As the pleasure became almost too much to bear Heather longed to touch him in return, to learn the hard contours of his body, and yet fear of rejection and remembered scorn held her back, her body on fire and about to be consumed in the flames.

Daniel moved against her restlessly, velvet encasing hard pleasure, his body curved into hers.

'I can't stand it any more!' she choked finally. 'Daniel, let me touch you!'

He slowly raised his head to look at her,

frowning as he saw the fevered longing in her over-bright eyes.

'I *need* to touch you,' she sobbed without defence.

'God, woman, you didn't have to——' He shook his head in bewilderment. 'I didn't mean I *never* wanted you to touch me,' he groaned, as he realised last night's rejection was the reason for her reluctance. 'Here,' he took her hand and guided it to him, drawing in a sharp breath as the soft caress of her hand closed about him. 'Don't ever stop!' he moaned as he fell back against the bed, taking her with him, capturing her breast between his teeth as she bent over him.

She was inexperienced, an innocent, and yet she knew instinctively the rhythm to drive Daniel wild, hesitating only as he thrashed wildly beneath her.

His lids flew wide, his eyes silver-grey. 'For God's sake, don't stop!' he choked fiercely.

Their kisses were wild, their caresses wilder, totally out of control, and yet, even through the sensual haze, Heather was aware enough to tense as Daniel probed the moisture between her thighs, although she welcomed the pain that was to come if it meant she had the pleasure of belonging to him completely, sure that once that barrier had been breached they would know the ultimate pleasure together.

He was demanding entry to a door that had never been opened, his hips thrusting forward as his hands beneath her buttocks pulled her

up on to him. The tearing pain left her open
to accommodate him and, as she had instinctively known, he surged inside to fill her
completely.

He lay still above her, breathing raggedly.
'Are you all right?'

'Yes,' she assured him quickly.

He trailed kisses down her cheek and throat
until he reached the dusky-rose nipple that
pleaded for his lips and tongue. 'Lift yourself
into me,' he groaned in a husky plea.

She cupped her breast, offering it to him,
breathing her satisfaction as he claimed it
roughly. The erotic pleasure-pain of Daniel's
teeth and tongue tugging rhythmically on the
sensitive bud made her forget the stinging pain
between her thighs, as he began to move slowly
against her with measured strokes. By the time
he released her throbbing breast to claim her
mouth, the pain between her thighs had turned
to a warm ache that quickly threatened to
consume her.

'Daniel . . . Oh, Daniel!' She gripped his
shoulders as she arched against him in frenzied
need, their bodies hot and damp, hard and
soft, aching for completion. And then the need
was appeased, and she felt Daniel tense inside
her as the flames and sparks of fulfilment
captured her and took her to a mindless cocoon
of pleasure, leaving her weak and gasping even
as she realised he had reached his own warm
pulsating pleasure.

Heather felt weak and exhausted, but so

very much alive, sensitised in every nerve-ending. 'When can we do it again?' she asked breathlessly.

He frowned. 'Didn't you——?'

'Oh yes, I did.' Colour heightened her cheeks. 'That's why I want to do it again!'

Daniel's chest moved slightly above her as he laughed softly. 'When would you *like* to do it again?'

'Now,' she told him without inhibition, sure she had discovered paradise. 'Do you think—oh . . . !'

'Yes, I *think*,' he groaned as he began to surge inside her. His expression was suddenly serious. 'Are you sure you're up to this?' He searched the flushed beauty of her face. 'No!' he cursed harshly as uncertainty clouded her eyes, her smile fading. 'I'm never going to ridicule you in bed again,' he promised gruffly. 'I meant, aren't you—too sore?'

Mischief lightened her eyes as she moved provocatively against him. 'No, I don't believe I am.'

His mouth quirked. 'Neither do I. God, Heather, do that again,' he encouraged as she slowly thrust against him. 'Again! And again! And, oh God, again!' His body convulsed time after time with the pleasure she was giving him.

Their second time together was even wilder than the first, their joy in each other as ecstatic and, as Heather drifted off to sleep in Daniel's arms, she was convinced she had found heaven.

But with love only on her side of the relationship, how long could heaven last?

CHAPTER EIGHT

Two days.

Two days of peaceful harmony, three nights of undreamt of sensual pleasure. And now this! Heather had believed Daniel was at last coming to care for her, but today had proved how wrong she was. He couldn't have devised a worse torture than this.

'Settling in OK?'

She blinked back the tears of disillusionment as she looked up to meet her uncle's warm gaze. 'Fine, thanks,' she smiled blankly.

He grinned, coming further into the room. 'You'll soon get used to the routine here.'

She would never 'get used' to being here! She wasn't cut out to work at Air International, she had no idea what people were talking about most of the time, despite having grown up with the business very much a part of her life.

Daniel had insisted she leave the house with him this morning, and imagining he had some surprise in mind, she had excitedly agreed. Nothing had prepared her for his announcement on the drive over here that he had arranged an office and a secretary for her at Air International, bursting the bubble of euphoria she had been existing in with one blow. What did she know about running an airline, running an *office* for that matter? And Daniel had known just how far out of her depth she would be.

She knew why he had done it, of course. She had been getting too close, becoming too much like the wife he had never really wanted. And he had chosen exactly the right way to show her how inadequate she was to share any of his life.

They had spent the last two evenings at home, had got along surprisingly well together, and the nights had been pure enchantment, all awkwardness gone between them as they sought only to give each other pleasure. Daniel's only acknowledgement of her innocence had been his brief concern after their first lovemaking; he had never mentioned the subject again. But he had continued to treat her with tenderness and consideration in bed.

And now this!

If she hadn't been feeling so angry at this effort to humiliate her she would have cried in earnest. But she was too furious to do that. If Daniel thought he could make a fool of her, he was going to find she wouldn't give him the satisfaction!

She stood up, picking up her clutch-bag. 'I have no intention of doing that, Uncle Lionel,' she informed him lightly. 'So whoever Daniel threw out of this office to accommodate me

can move back in again any time they want
to!'

'Heather?'

She turned briefly in the doorway, her
expression softening as she saw her uncle's
bewilderment. 'If Daniel should ask where I've
gone, you could tell him I have to see about
the delivery of some furniture today.'

'But——'

Her mouth twisted. 'I'm sure he'll understand.'

Lionel shook his head. 'I'm not sure I do.'
He looked totally dazed.

'I was getting too close, Uncle Lionel,'
Heather sighed. 'This is Daniel's way of putting
me firmly back in my place.'

He crossed the room to join her. 'I thought
the marriage was working out . . . ?'

'It was,' she nodded. 'That's why I'm being
put in my place.' She sighed again. 'Daniel has
nothing to worry about, I won't forget again.'
How could she forget, after this, that no matter
how much physical pleasure she gave him
Daniel would never allow her to be his *life's*
partner?

'Darling, let me take you to lunch so that
we can talk about——'

'It's only ten-thirty,' she reminded him drily.
'Besides, I'm fine,' she assured him. 'I learnt
to suffer Daniel's indifference, or total cruelty,
a long time ago,' she added bitterly, knowing
he had never hurt her quite as badly as this
before.

'I'm sure you must have misunderstood Daniel's motives.' Her uncle still frowned. 'He assured me when he moved Phillip out of here that——'

'Now I know this is all Daniel's idea of a sick joke!' she scorned. 'Where did he put Phillip?'

'He's in with Bob Hayes,' her uncle revealed with some reluctance. 'But he assured us all that it's only temporary——'

'Of course he did—he knew Phillip's office would soon be vacant again!' She grimaced. 'I think he may have pushed me too far.'

Lionel looked worried. 'What do you mean?'

She shrugged. 'Just because Daddy didn't approve of women having a career, and I've never used my qualifications for that purpose, it doesn't mean that I don't have any. Maybe I will find myself a job, as that seems to be what Daniel wants. Or maybe I'll set up my own company. I certainly have the money now.'

'Darling, talk to Daniel first——'

'I don't need his permission!' Her eyes flashed. 'He thinks I'm a useless butterfly, but he's about to learn differently.'

'Of course you don't need his permission,' her uncle soothed. 'I wasn't suggesting that you did. But I'm sure you must have misunderstood Daniel's reasons for bringing you in here——'

'How can I have done that when they're so glaringly obvious? I tried to tell myself I was wrong about this as soon as he told me, but he just dumped me in this office half an hour ago and disappeared.' Heather scowled. 'He knew I had no idea of the intricacies of running an airline, but he hoped I'd have a stumbling go at it, if only to show me I have no business being here.'

'I'm sure you're wrong——'

'He told me the other night exactly how he felt about my owning half *his* airline,' she remembered bitterly. 'I should never have let myself forget that.' Her head went back proudly. 'I won't again.' No matter how much she still desired him physically.

'He can be a hard man,' her uncle shook his head, 'but not that hard, I'm sure.'

Heather's mouth twisted. 'I appreciate your loyalty to him—but I doubt if he does. He uses people up, Uncle Lionel, and when they're of no further use to him he discards them!'

He gave a slight smile. 'I think you're being melodramatic, darling, because at the moment you're angry with him.'

'I'm past anger now.' And, strangely enough, she was. Now she was just numb. Something delicate and fragile had grown between them the last few days and nights, an emotion that needed to be nurtured and treated gently if it were to survive, and Daniel had deliberately trampled on it. All she could think of now was that it was a terrible waste. 'Don't let him hurt you, too, Uncle Lionel.' She put her hand on his arm.

He looked taken aback by the warning. 'What on earth do you mean?'

'He means for Air International to be completely his.' Heather gave a sad shake of her head. 'And he doesn't like it when people get in his way.'

'I'm not in his way, love.' Her uncle patted her arm. 'And I'll be retiring soon.'

'You're young yet——'

He shook his head. 'I've only stayed on this long to give Daniel a chance to find his bearings after Max's death. I'm fifty-five now, and I have enough money of my own not to have to worry about it any more. Besides, I have a wife I'd like to spend more time with,' he added wryly.

Heather had a feeling that the time for him being with Stella had long gone, the other woman had gone her own way now, having taken lovers for years as far as she could see. But maybe if her uncle were at home more that would stop. She hoped so, for his sake!

But she couldn't help feeling that it was Daniel's need for complete domination over Air International that was forcing her uncle out of the company; he had never talked about retirement when her father was still alive. Daniel had a need to own, to possess completely, and it didn't allow for anyone else's feelings.

Seeing Stella dropping Phillip off outside the office building did little to increase her confidence that her uncle giving up work would help his marriage. Surely the two of them weren't——? But why not? Stella had shown a preference for Phillip on several occasions that she knew of, and what did it matter that he was several years her junior?

'Leaving so soon?' Phillip mocked as they met outside on the pavement.

'Just arriving?' Heather returned as sarcastically.

'As it happens, yes,' he drawled without remorse. 'I had an early appointment this morning.'

Her cheeks flushed as she wished she could rebuke him for his tardiness, if not for seeing Stella when her husband had already left for work. And yet she had just revoked her right to give any of Air International's employees a rebuke of any kind. 'Your office is ready for you to move back into any time *you're* ready,' she bit out.

'My God!' He gave a choked laugh of disbelief. 'You didn't last long, did you?'

'I didn't "last" at all,' she returned stiffly. 'I decided my husband's generous offer of a working partnership wasn't to my liking.'

Some of the resentful anger drained out of him. 'Are you really happy with him, Heather?'

'I'm happy enough,' she dismissed. 'Do you think it's wise to see Stella?' she prompted gently.

Phillip instantly stiffened. 'My private life is none of your business now—is it?' he challenged.

'No,' she sighed. 'But I wouldn't like to see my uncle hurt.'

His eyes widened. 'Are you threatening me?'

A blush darkened her cheeks as she recalled what had happened the last time a threat of hers had been taken seriously; Daniel had proved very effectively his reaction to threats! 'Of course not,' she dismissed sharply. 'Just stating a fact. My uncle loves his wife very much, you know.'

He shrugged. 'I can't be held responsible for Stella's infidelity——'

'You didn't have to accept her offer!' Heather glared.

He sighed. 'She's never made any secret of the fact that she finds me attractive, and with you out of my life——'

'Don't blame me for your weakness, Phillip,' she snapped. 'At least take responsibility for what you've done.'

'The only thing I've done is accept a beautiful woman into my bed——'

'A beautiful *married* woman!'

'A person is only married as long as they want to be. Maybe you should bear that in mind, Heather,' he added softly.

She paled. Daniel's efforts to humiliate her today had been so transparent! 'My marriage is none of your concern,' she hissed.

His mouth twisted mockingly. 'I'm not even sure it's any of yours!'

With one last cold glare into his handsome face she stepped to the edge of the pavement and hailed a taxi, grateful when one stopped almost instantly, her legs shaking badly as she sat down, and leaned forward to give the driver the address of the new house.

Organising the furniture in the bedrooms kept her busy until lunchtime when the men told her they would be back in an hour to bring in the furniture for the master bedroom. Heather had a feeling they were going off to the pub a couple of miles down the road that had quite a good reputation for lunches.

It really was going to be a beautiful house, she thought, as she wandered from room to room, not in the least interested in eating lunch herself.

A noise on the stairs made her turn towards the door. 'Did you forget——?' Her light greeting ended abruptly, her smile fading and her expression hardening, as she saw it was Daniel standing in the doorway.

'Expecting someone?' he taunted, his eyes glittering coldly.

Her brows arched. 'Just the men to finish bringing in the furniture,' she returned as coldly. 'As you can see, they haven't done this room yet.' The midnight-blue carpet of the master bedroom made Daniel's eyes look almost as dark.

'You didn't think I might be Wingate?' he ground out.

'I doubt that he even knows about this house, let alone intends meeting me here,' she snapped.

'You were talking to him outside earlier,' Daniel accused. 'I saw the two of you together.'

She couldn't prevent the guilty colour that flooded her cheeks, even though Stella and Phillip were the guilty ones. 'I spoke to him, yes.' Her head was back defiantly. 'I wasn't aware that was a crime?'

'It isn't.' Daniel strode into the room with deceptive casualness. 'What are you doing here?'

'Surely that's obvious.' She faced him challengingly.

His mouth twisted. 'I doubt if your presence here today was of paramount importance to the furniture people!'

That he was right caused a flush in her cheeks. 'I sent home the maid who had come over to supervise them,' she admitted.

'Why?'

Heather shrugged, aware that mentally they were circling around each other, warily waiting for the other to strike. Although she doubted if Daniel faced anyone warily, he appeared to be always in complete control, of himself and the situation. 'I chose the furniture, I wanted to see it arranged in the places I'd chosen for it.' The majority of furniture from her father's home was being sold off; to have brought it here would just have been to transport the bad memories with her.

'Didn't you have a prior commitment this morning?'

She didn't even blink in the face of the

deceptively mild question. 'Nothing of any urgency,' she dismissed steadily.

Daniel drew in a ragged breath. 'No?' he grated.

She shook her head. 'Nothing that comes to mind.'

The tension between them was a tangible thing. But Heather was determined not to be the one to back down. Daniel was only angry because his plan to humiliate her into realising how useless she was hadn't been allowed time to work.

Suddenly something snapped inside him, his hands painfully gripping her arms. 'What the hell do you mean by walking out on me in that way?' His eyes glittered angrily.

She met his gaze unflinchingly. 'Disappointed I didn't *run* out?' she returned tautly.

'I gave you the opportunity of a full partnership at AI and you——'

'You gave me a chance to make an idiot of myself!' She pulled away from him, even though the movement hurt her arms. 'I'm sorry I didn't hang around to give you that satisfaction!' she added sarcastically.

His eyes narrowed . 'You didn't give yourself, or us, time to adjust——'

'And I don't intend to!' She looked at him challengingly. 'Not for your amusement or anyone else's!'

'I don't know what the hell you're talking about.' He shook his head impatiently.

'Don't you?' she derided harshly. 'Maybe I

have been a little dazzled by your physical expertise the last few days, but I'm not completely stupid!'

'You aren't stupid at all. That's why I——'

'Why you decided to humiliate me into realising I can never have anything but a financial interest in Air International? Well, you needn't worry any more, Daniel,' she snapped. 'I *have* no other interest than that in the airline, and as long as you make sure my share of the profits goes into my bank account I don't want to know about *your* airline.'

'Our physical relationship is enough for you, is it?' he scorned.

Heather had believed it was something to build upon, the start of a deeper relationship, but she couldn't make love with a man who held her in such contempt. 'I don't even want that any more——'

'Well, *I* do,' he rasped coldly.

'What's the matter, Daniel?' she taunted. 'Aren't you *bored* yet?'

'Not by a long way,' he assured her grimly. 'And to prove it . . . !'

Why couldn't love die at will? she thought abstractedly as Daniel lowered her on to the carpeted floor and made love to her with a familiarity that had her weak with longing within seconds rather than minutes.

At first she moved her head from side to side in an effort to stop his mouth claiming hers, but Daniel just grasped her chin as he slowly plundered her lips.

Her clothing was impatiently removed from her, and she cried out as Daniel's hot mouth drew one aching nipple inside the warm cavern. They had discovered together that her breasts were the most sensitised part of her body, and Daniel didn't relinquish them until she was weak and clinging to him, gasping her pleasure as he thrust inside her, meeting the fierce movements of his naked body with a demand of her own.

When they were together like this there was no room in her thoughts or body for anything but Daniel and the magic he created with her senses. Not even the fierceness of his expression could detract from the pleasure they found in each other's arms, and they reached the very essence of fulfilment together before Daniel collapsed weakly against her.

The weakness passed quickly, and he was scowling as he drew himself away from her. '*This* is mine,' he told her savagely, cupping her breast. 'And if you cease to be my wife before I'm ready for it I'll divorce you!' He stood up to begin pulling on his clothes.

Heather stared up at him, her hair a midnight cascade against the dark carpet, her face flushed, her lips bare of gloss. 'But you would lose your precious airline then,' she reminded him hardily.

'I'd probably be the major shareholder,' he shrugged. 'But you would lose everything. Is it worth denying me what you really want to give to risk that?'

She frowned. 'Why would you risk it?' Her voice was husky.

Any hopes she might have had concerning his feelings for her were dashed by his answer.

'I paid a high price for the use of your body.' He was fully clothed now, not a crease or speck of dust on the immaculately tailored, blue pin-striped suit and light blue shirt to show the intensity of the passion he had just shared with her. 'I never pay for anything I don't intend to make full use of!'

Another leftover hurt from his childhood. But she couldn't let compassion for his unorthodox upbringing deflect from the fact that he had set out to hurt and humiliate her—and that he had succeeded.

'We both paid the same price, Daniel,' she bit out. 'Although perhaps I paid a little more.'

His eyes narrowed. 'In what way?'

'You might not want to admit it, Daniel, but we both know I had no other lover before you, that your accusations about Phillip have always been completely unfounded.'

'Maybe that will change now,' he rasped.

'Maybe it will,' she taunted.

Daniel came down on one knee beside her, clasping a handful of her hair. 'I wouldn't advise it,' he grated.

'I don't believe I asked for your advice.' She faced him fearlessly.

'Don't do it, Heather,' he warned softly. 'You would regret it.'

She gave a slow smile. 'From what several

of my friends have told me about Phillip I don't think I would regret it at all.'

Daniel's hand tightened briefly in her hair before flinging it away from him as if she burnt him. 'The same friends who warned you against marrying me, I have no doubt,' he snapped.

Heather had never allowed anyone to say anything against Daniel in her presence, and she wasn't about to start now, no matter how unhappy he had made her. 'No doubt,' she drawled. 'Shouldn't you be getting back to work, Daniel?' she mocked. 'After all, I think one of us should be there.'

'I should have known you wouldn't be willing to work,' he spat out contemptuously. 'To soil your delicate little hands with real work. You are a Danvers, after all!'

She nodded coolly. 'And we've always been better at spending money than making it.'

'Your father proved that,' he scorned.

'But you're in charge now, Daniel, and I have complete confidence in your ability to run Air International,' she taunted, laughing softly as he strode furiously out of the room. ''Bye, Daniel,' she called as he slammed out of the house.

She refused to allow the tears to fall. She wouldn't give in to the desolation his contempt made her feel.

CHAPTER NINE

IT TOOK weeks rather than the days Heather had hoped to get her business even partially off the ground.

She had plenty of contacts, it was getting people to take her seriously that was the problem. She was Heather Danvers-Taggart, who had no reason to work for a living, and no one seemed to understand why she would want to. Then a friend gave her her first commission, and after that there didn't seem to be any shortage of people requiring her services.

Life with Daniel went on as never before. He left for work earlier in the mornings because of the longer drive into London, and he was usually later home for the same reason. His evenings were spent in his study after sharing a meal with her, and it was only when they went to bed that they communicated at all, and that was on a purely physical level. Daniel didn't ask her about her days, and she didn't volunteer the information either, and so he never knew that she spent almost every day away from the house doing a job she was growing to love.

She was a little disconcerted when she

arrived home at her usual five o'clock one evening, a couple of months into their marriage, to find that Daniel had arrived home shortly after lunch. She ran upstairs to change before facing him in the lounge. Shilton had told her that he had asked where she was, but luckily the elderly man had no idea where she had been all day.

'You're back early today,' she ventured lightly. Daniel's expression, once he had lowered the newspaper he had been reading, was not encouraging.

'Yes,' he snapped.

She raised her brows, moving to rearrange an already perfect vase of roses. 'Anything wrong?' she lightly tried again.

'Should there be?' he snapped, narrowed eyes following her every move.

Heather shrugged. 'You don't usually get home in the middle of the day.'

'No.'

She sighed, holding on to her temper with difficulty. Surprisingly enough, Daniel was still a gentle and considerate lover, although his manner the rest of the time still left a lot to be desired. 'Why did you come home early, Daniel?' she asked bluntly.

'Why shouldn't I?' he rasped. 'This *is* my home.'

She drew in a deep controlling breath. 'If you don't want to talk about it . . . ' She turned to leave.

'There *is* nothing to discuss about my

coming home early for a change.' He surged to his feet. 'But I would be interested to know where you've been spending your days lately.'

Heather froze, turning slowly. 'Shilton told you I've—been out a lot?'

'Not a lot, every day!' Daniel corrected harshly. 'Where have you been, Heather?'

She managed what she hoped was a nonchalant shrug. 'Just out.'

'Doing what?' His eyes were steely slits.

'Meeting friends. Shopping——'

'*Every* day?' he scorned disbelievingly.

'Why not?' she retorted coldly. 'I believe we agreed that spending money is what I do best!'

Daniel's mouth was tight. 'And these friends you've been meeting, are they male or female?'

She relaxed a little as he transferred his attention to that part of her answer. 'Female —mostly,' she supplied provocatively.

'And would one of these male *friends* be Wingate?'

'If Phillip has been guilty of not being at work when he should be, it certainly isn't because of me,' she snapped. 'The last I heard he'd got over his disappointment concerning me.'

'Stella?' rasped Daniel.

'You would have to ask him about that.' She evaded condemning the other woman, not sure if the affair had continued all this time or not. If it had it would be a first; Stella's affairs seemed to be as fleeting as they were meaningless.

'I dismissed him,' Daniel revealed gratingly.
Her eyes widened. 'When?'

'I would have thought you would have
known about it,' he derided.

'I told you, I haven't seen Phillip for some
time,' she bit out forcefully.

Daniel shrugged. 'I asked him to leave
several weeks ago; he was happy to go,' he
mocked.

Heather had had no idea. But then, after
that disastrous morning at Air International
all those weeks ago she hadn't been near the
place. And she had been so busy launching
her business too . . .

'Why?' she frowned.

Daniel's mouth twisted. 'Don't you think
he'd given me more than enough reason?'

She shrugged. 'That didn't seem to bother
you at the time.'

'It doesn't bother me now, either,' he rasped.
'I just don't want anyone working at AI who
isn't completely loyal to me and the company.'

'The company must come first,' she taunted,
mimicking a salute.

'Not at all,' Daniel snapped. 'It was his
comments about my wife that I found unac-
ceptable.'

Heather's eyes widened, deep purple, fringed
by thick dark lashes. 'You were defending me?'
It didn't come as any surprise that Phillip had
made derogatory comments about her, he was
still very bitter about the end of their relationship, and had made no secret of the fact.

Daniel's reaction to it *did* surprise her, though.

'You do happen to be my wife,' he nodded abruptly.

'But——'

'When I was a child I had no answer to the comments made about my mother and the men who visited her,' he explained coldly. 'And believe me, there were plenty of comments made! But I'm *married* to Heather Danvers, a woman with an impeccable reputation and bloodline,' he scorned. 'Of course I defended you!'

She had always known that *who* she was had made marrying her a sweeter pill to swallow, and that was partly why she had never told Daniel that Max hadn't really been her father. The other part, of course, was that she would never be able to tell Daniel half the truth, and admitting the extent of her father's hatred for her was something she found hard to do.

'Thank you,' she replied coolly. 'Even if that does make me feel more like a brood mare than a woman.'

Daniel's eyes narrowed on the slender length of her body. 'You aren't——?'

'No,' she dismissed harshly.

'No doubt you've had time to reconsider having *my* children and are taking the necessary steps to prevent them.' His mouth twisted with bitterness.

Her eyes flashed. 'No, I'm not taking the "necessary steps" to prevent a pregnancy! My

God, you may not like other people making comments about your wife, but you certainly have no compunction in throwing every insult at me yourself!'

'Heather——'

'I *want* a child. It will be someone of my own to love,' she added harshly. 'Someone who will love me for myself, and not judge me because my name was Danvers or because I'm not what people expect me to be!' She was breathing hard in her agitation. Why couldn't her father, and now Daniel, accept her for what she was, and have loved her in spite of it?

'Heather, I didn't mean——'

'Of course that's what you meant.' She blinked back the tears that wouldn't be denied. 'You think I'm as shallow as all those other people who can't see you're better than any of them! Well, I *can* see, Daniel. I can understand the single-minded determination inside you that made you the successful man you are today. I know exactly how hard you must have worked to overcome the background you must often have felt would suffocate you. Well, the wealth and success are yours now, Daniel, but you're still making everyone else pay for the fact that your mother supported the two of you in the only way she could. Your mother wasn't a whore, Daniel,' she told him heatedly. 'If she was, there are thousands of other woman, married and unmarried, who are just like her!'

He stood very still. 'It's difficult to trust anyone when you've known taunts and condescension most of your life.'

She could have wept for the desolation of the admission, for the fact that he had been able to admit it at all. 'I know that,' she soothed. 'I do know that,' she insisted firmly. 'But I have no wish to hurt you, Daniel, I just want our marriage to be a success. That's all! We were forced into this marriage by circumstances, but wouldn't it serve my father right if we could be happy together?'

He gave the ghost of a smile at her vehemence. 'It would—but I doubt if it's possible.'

She sighed heavily, her shoulders drooping dejectedly. Well, she had tried. 'If you'll excuse me, I think I'll go and lie down for a while; I have a headache.' And a heartache that would never go away!

He put out a hand towards her. 'Heather, I——' He broke off abruptly, shaking his head as he turned away.

She was used to people turning away from her, the man she had thought was her father had done it all of her life, and her marriage to Daniel had been doomed to failure, she had always known that. Then why did she suddenly feel so alone?

She had *wanted* this marriage to work in spite of its bad beginning, she just hadn't known how to overcome Daniel's mistrust of the softer emotions, and because of that, she had allowed herself to become exactly the type of woman he despised. Who was she trying to fool? Daniel despised *all* women!

She quickly pulled on a robe over her nakedness as a knock sounded on the bedroom door, smiling at Shilton as he hesitated in the doorway.

'Mr Taggart told me you have a headache,' he said awkwardly. 'I took the liberty of bringing up a cup of your usual hot chocolate.'

Her smile was rueful as she invited him in. 'Just like old times, isn't it?' she sighed, remembering other headaches she had 'developed' just to escape from her father's barbs.

The elderly man gave her a frowning look. 'I hope not, Miss Heather.' He used her old form of address in his distress.

Heather gave him a quizzical look. Shilton had been an unobtrusive part of her life for as long as she could remember, a quietly thoughtful man who seemed able to anticipate her needs often before she realised them herself. Maybe because he was always there, so unassuming, she had never realised how much he must have known of the happenings in her father's house all these years. Max had been so careful, while he was alive, to hide his real feelings towards her from his friends that neither of them had realised Shilton—and probably the other household staff, too—knew exactly how he had felt about her. And, as Shilton had been with her father long before he married her mother, the elderly man might even know the true facts behind her birth.

'It isn't,' she gently reassured him, knowing he was genuinely fond of her. 'This headache is very real.' Her gaze moved past him as she saw Daniel standing in the doorway.

Shilton turned to look at him, too, quietly excusing himself.

Daniel strode into the room. 'What was all that about?'

Heather shrugged, turning away. 'Shilton was just concerned about me.'

'Meaning I'm not?' he rasped.

She sighed, too weary for another battle. 'I didn't mean that at all. You——'

'I'm sorry.' He put up his hands defensively, giving a self-disgusted shake of his head. 'I came up here to apologise, not start another argument with you.' His mouth quirked as her eyes widened. 'Yes, I do know how to apologise,' he mocked lightly. 'And at the moment I have so much to apologise for I don't know where to start!'

'Daniel——'

'Are you still interested in why I came home early today?' He raised dark brows.

She became suddenly still. 'Of course I am,' she nodded tensely.

He shrugged. 'We can't go on like this. We'll end up hating each other.'

'I thought you already did hate me.'

Pain clouded his eyes. 'Of course I don't hate you, damn it! Do I make love to you as if I hate you? Do I——'

'Daniel,' she cut in softly.

'Sorry,' he muttered. 'But it was a damned stupid thing to say,' he rasped. 'I like you. I certainly admire your spirit in standing up to me the way that you do,' he added ruefully.

'I'm glad you realise it takes courage,' she said drily.

His mouth quirked. 'I know what a bastard I can be, no one better—because I'm just as hard on myself as I am on everyone else.'

'Harder,' Heather put in softly.

'Maybe,' he acknowledged abruptly, running a hand through the thickness of his hair. 'But I came home early today to see if we couldn't at least talk out some of the problems we have in our marriage, starting with an explanation of why I wanted you to work with me at AI.'

'I know your reason for that——'

'No, you don't,' he snapped impatiently. 'You're a very intelligent woman—sometimes,' he added pointedly. 'You showed me how interested you were in AI, you were furious with me when I dealt with that bomb scare alone. I thought you might actually like to take an active part in your own company!'

'That's why you just dumped me in that office and disappeared——'

'I didn't *dump* you anywhere,' he rasped. 'An emergency came up that I had to deal with, but I was coming back to spend the day with you in *your* office. By the time I returned you had already left, leaving me a message about having to organise the delivery of some furniture!'

'You certainly hadn't given the impression you would welcome my presence at Air International.' Heather defended her actions; what else could she have thought?

'We had become close in those first days after our marriage, closer than I've ever been to anyone else,' he revealed grimly. 'I wanted to *share* the excitement of running AI with you!'

'Well, how was I supposed to know that?' Her eyes flashed.

'Because it——Hell, we're arguing again.' Daniel sighed his impatience. 'Will you give the idea some thought now?' he asked evenly. 'We can work together to build it even better and bigger than it already is.' His eyes glowed with the challenge.

Heather knew the full significance of the offer, knew that Daniel had always preferred to walk through life alone. If only he had explained all this two months ago! 'I'm afraid it's too late for that——'

'My God, one thing I never thought about you was that you would bear a grudge for every *imagined* slight,' he scowled.

'I didn't *imagine* the fact that you put me in the office of the man you had believed was my lover!'

'I knew by then that he wasn't and never had been,' he reminded her harshly. 'I gave you that office because it was the one closest to mine without my having to ask Lionel to move out!'

'I'm surprised you didn't do that,' she snapped caustically. 'As it is he's thinking of retiring early when he had never even mentioned the idea before you took over!'

Daniel's mouth twisted. 'Maybe he'll reconsider that decision if he has his beloved niece at AI, too!'

'I told you, it's too late for that.' She shook her head.

'Because of some damned grudge you have no right——'

'Because I already *have* a job!' she corrected heatedly, unable to believe this had really started out as a conciliatory conversation.

'You *what*?' Daniel's voice cracked between them like a whip.

Heather met his gaze unflinchingly. 'I have a job,' she repeated calmly.

'Doing what?' His voice was so soft that its very control was dangerous.

'I own and run an interior design company. Don't look so sceptical, Daniel,' she snapped at his derisive snort. 'I do have all the necessary qualifications, I've just never had the opportunity to use them before.' It had all started out as a way of showing him that even though she was out of her depth at Air International she knew exactly what she was doing with the interiors of houses and offices. It had started out that way, but in the weeks since it had become so much more; she loved what she was doing, got up every morning with the challenge of a new day. 'Didn't I do a wonderful job on the interior of this house?' she prompted lightly as Daniel still looked thunderstruck.

'How many people know about this business of yours?' he rasped.

She frowned, shaking her head. 'I don't know what you mean.'

'Who knows you own this interior design company?' he enlarged harshly.

'All my friends, the ones I've been asking for business, anyway,' she grinned. 'And quite a lot of other people too. I'm really enjoying it——'

'So half of London is aware of the fact that my wife works for a living?' he cut in savagely, his eyes glittering silver.

'You wanted me to work at AI—'

'That's different and you know it!' he snapped fiercely.

'No,' she frowned, 'I don't know it. What's so wrong with my doing something I love so much?'

She had envisaged triumphantly telling him of her success in a few more months, once the company was well established; she certainly hadn't imagined this as his reaction. Amazement, perhaps, that she had managed to achieve so much in so little time, because she had achieved a lot already, had taken on two new designers to the staff of five she had already had at the failing company she had taken over.

'Or are you more like my father than I

realised?' she accused. 'Not liking to see others enjoying their life, but taking delight in denying them the things you know they want?'

'I'm nothing like Max, and you know it——'

'I believed you weren't——'

'I'm not,' Daniel rasped firmly. 'But there's no reason for you to go out to work.'

'There's every reason—I'm enjoying it,' she told him stubbornly. 'For the first time in my life I feel independent, free.'

'You're my wife!' He glared.

'Have I been any less your wife the last two months than I was for those few days before I started my business?' she challenged.

A ruddy hue darkened his cheeks. 'You know that wasn't what I meant!'

'No,' she sighed, 'I don't think I do know. I don't understand your reaction at all.'

His hands clenched at his sides. 'When your father was alive you were quite content to stay at home and run his household for him.'

'Who says I was?' Her eyes flashed. 'I wasn't given a choice.'

'You were an adult——'

'Completely dominated by Max Danvers,' she recalled bitterly. 'You saw by his will how much he cared about my happiness; I tried all my life to gain his approval, to find some way of making him love me. And I gave up a lot of things that it would have made me happy to do.'

'A career?'

'Yes!' She looked at him imploringly. 'It's

something I always wanted, something I've always loved, but the closest my father would let me come to it was allowing me to decorate his home. All he ever wanted from me was that I always be there, always beautiful, always attentive to his needs. Is that what you want from me, too?' she asked in a pained voice.

'Doesn't it bother you that people are probably laughing at us behind our backs?' he grated. 'Saying that I can't even support my wife!'

A heavy weight settled on her chest. 'It obviously bothers you. Why, Daniel? A lot of women have careers nowadays, regardless of wealth.'

'Not *my* wife!' he stormed.

'That's the real problem, isn't it, Daniel?' she sighed. 'It isn't that I've at last found something that makes me happy, it isn't even that I chose to do this rather than work with you at Air International, it's because *your* wife is working, something I'm sure you once swore to yourself would never happen.'

'Right,' he agreed tersely.

'Like my father, you're only thinking of this from your own point of view, how it affects you,' she said heavily. 'You don't care about the fact that this makes me happy.'

'You were happy before!'

'No, I wasn't!' she cried frustratedly. 'I've always wanted something *more* in my life!'

He drew in a ragged breath. 'Then you refuse to give up this business?'

'Yes!'

A nerve pulsed in his cheek. 'Even though you know exactly how important it is to me?'

'Oh, Daniel,' she shook her head sadly, 'it's just as important to me that I *do* work.'

'Very well,' he nodded stiffly, wrenching open the door. 'You've made your choice.'

What choice? Heather stared numbly at the door after he had closed it. *What* choice had she just made?

By the time she was able to move to open the bedroom door she was just in time to hear the front door close decisively behind Daniel. He had gone. But where? And for how long?

He had promised to give this marriage two months, and that time was now up. Did that mean he would return to the life he had led before their marriage, to his other women, something she knew he hadn't done in the last two months despite their arguments, too busy to see anyone else during the day, and spending every night with her? Had he gone to another woman now?

Tears squeezed between her tightly closed lids. She had just wanted something of her own, something she could finally claim was her own success. Was that so wrong? She understood Daniel's aversion to having a working wife, of course she did, but he was making no effort to see this from her point of view.

Was this it, then, the end of the dreams she

had had of this marriage one day being a happy one?

If giving up her business would give them that, then she wouldn't have hesitated to do it. But she couldn't see anything changing the way things were between herself and Daniel in the near future, least of all making herself unhappy and resentful.

Daniel still hadn't returned to the house by the time she went to bed, and she stared blindly at the ceiling as she wondered who he was with. Any number of women would have been glad of his attention, in fact several of her friends had confided recently how much they envied her her husband rather than pitied her, as Daniel had always accused. She had blushingly accepted their compliments about her husband; now she couldn't help wishing he wasn't quite so attractive, that his air of needing no one wasn't quite such a challenge to every woman he met.

Quite apart from that she missed his presence beside her in their bed. Rarely a night had gone by when he hadn't made love to her, and the closeness between them then was all she had to comfort her when he was so much apart from her at other times.

She was staring fixedly at the bedroom door, had been for some time, when it was quietly opened and she could see Daniel step into the room.

It was one o'clock in the morning, she had no idea where he had been or who he had been with, but she was so glad to see him at all that she didn't care about that right now, giving a choked sob as she held out her arms to him.

For a moment he froze. And then he was crossing the room in long strides, coming down on his knees beside the bed to cradle her in his arms. 'I'm sorry,' he groaned between raining kisses on her cheeks and brows. 'I'm so sorry!'

For a moment it felt as if her heart would break as she guessed the reason for his apology, and then it didn't matter any more as Daniel kissed *her* as if he would never stop. What did it matter who he had been with tonight, he had come back to *her*!

'No, darling, no!' He shook his head as he guessed the reason for her brief resistance, staring down at her in the darkness. 'My only companion tonight was a brandy bottle, and then only briefly,' he added ruefully. 'Then I realised I'd been wrong to talk to you the way I did, to demand you give up something you love so much.'

'I love *you* Daniel.' Heather clung to him, her eyes bright with unshed tears, beyond pride now. She had tried everything else to try and make their marriage a success, and none of it had worked, and after going through the trauma tonight of believing she had lost him completely she just wanted him to know how she felt about him. 'If you really want me to stop working then I'll do it.'

His hand trembled slightly as he smoothed the hair at her temple. 'Wh-what did you say? About—about——'

She swallowed hard, knowing that Daniel had difficulty even saying the word. 'I love you, Daniel. I always have.'

'You had a crush——'

'Not a crush.' She shook her head. 'It was love, it always has been.'

His face was very white in the moonlight, his eyes darkly searching. 'Then Max's will——'

'Has nothing to do with how I feel about you,' she told him firmly. 'Except that it's made it impossible for you to ever take my love seriously. It's all right, Daniel,' she caressed his cheek as a nerve pulsed there, 'I don't expect you to believe me.'

'It isn't that——'

'I don't expect any declarations of love in return, either,' she sighed. 'I'm just tired of hiding my feelings behind a wall of cool sophistication. I loved you from the moment we first met, and nothing you do is ever going to change that.'

'I can be a bastard——'

'Rigid and self-defensive,' she corrected firmly. 'It's just part of the person you are, it doesn't change my love for you.'

'Heather, I—I——' He swallowed hard. 'Will you hold me?' He rested his head against her breasts. 'Just hold me!'

For ever, if he would let her!

It was the first time, the very first time, that she had felt close to him, that he had let her close to him, without them having made love first.

CHAPTER TEN

'I'M sorry, darling, but I'm afraid we could be a little late.'

The use of the endearment still thrilled Heather to her toes!

As she had assured Daniel that night a month ago, she wasn't expecting any declarations of love in return, and she hadn't received any, then or in the time since. But their relationship had changed. Daniel no longer spent all his evenings in his study. Occasionally he still brought work home, but when it did happen he invited Heather to join him and she would usually curl up in an armchair in there and read a book while he worked. He telephoned her at least once a day when he was at work, if only to tell her what time he would be home for dinner. He had even accepted her invitation to look around Taggart Interiors, offering a few helpful comments, but no more criticism. And at night he made love to her with a sweet desire that had her crying out her love for him as he drove her to the brink of madness. And lastly, he occasionally called her darling!

As he had just now. It certainly took the sting out of the fact that he and her uncle were going to be late for dinner tonight.

'I'm sure Stella and I will do our best to entertain each other until you arrive,' she said drily, anticipating the bitchiness the other woman would show in full measure without the slightly sobering presence of the two men. Her uncle and Stella had been over to dinner several times during the last three months, and each time the other woman seemed to become more scathing.

Daniel gave a throaty chuckle. 'Keep her away from the dinner table; the knives would be too accessible!'

Heather felt an inner glow at the complete naturalness of his laugh, no bitterness or scepticism in his manner with her now, as if he were finally beginning to believe in her love for him. They still had a long way to go, and she hadn't yet told him the truth about Max's relationship to her, but each new day gave her the confidence to feel they would soon have everything together.

'I'll try and hold her off until you get here,' she mocked.

'She's getting worse, isn't she?' he agreed, soberly.

It didn't surprise her that Daniel had noticed that, it would take a blind man not to notice how caustic the other woman had become. Although Uncle Lionel seemed completely unaware of his wife's brittle manner. Maybe he was just too close to the situation.

'I'm sure it will pass,' Heather dismissed.

'Now what time can I expect you home?'

'No later than eight-thirty,' he replied confidently.

'There's nothing wrong, is there?' she frowned; Daniel hadn't worked late at the office for weeks.

'Lionel has some figures we need to go through,' he explained. 'It shouldn't take too long.'

Heather was far from looking forward to being alone with Stella for half an hour. The two of them had little or nothing in common, and the other woman had been openly disparaging about Heather's career, scorning the need to work when she was already so wealthy, having spent years herself trying to get *away* from working. She lost no opportunity to get in as many rude comments about it as she could. Tonight proved to be no different.

'If I had your money I wouldn't waste my time working for other people,' she attacked.

Stella had greeted her by telling her how tired she looked, and the statement about her money had been made in answer to Heather's comment that she had been working hard.

Heather smiled. 'Could we at least go through to the lounge before you start an argument?' she said lightly.

The other woman gave a haughty inclination of her head; she was looking very attractive in a clinging black dress, showing by the slenderness of her figure that she had lost weight the last couple of months. In fact, she looked thinner than she had when Heather had seen her two weeks ago.

'Are you on a diet?' Heather frowned.

Blue eyes flashed. 'Of course not,' snapped Stella. 'There's absolutely nothing wrong with my figure.'

'I didn't mean to imply that there was——'

'*You've* put weight on,' the other woman accused.

She had, a little. Despite working harder than she ever had before, spending ecstatic nights in Daniel's arms, she had put several pounds on lately as the result of a suddenly healthy appetite. 'A few pounds,' she conceded.

Stella gave her a critical look. 'You aren't pregnant already, are you?'

It was difficult to hold on to her temper in the face of the personal question that was put as a criticism; she was more than a little disappointed that she wasn't yet expecting Daniel's child. 'No,' she bit out tautly.

'Don't tell me you actually *want* children?' Stella scorned. 'I know I made very sure I wouldn't have any unwanted brats.'

Heather blinked. 'How?'

'The usual way,' the other woman shrugged. 'Lionel wanted them, but I didn't, and so——It's just as well it never happened,' she rasped.

Heather looked at Stella searchingly. It was true that the other woman would have made an atrocious parent, but even so, it should have been a decision both partners made.

Although she doubted Stella would see it that way if she pointed that out to her.

'Are you still seeing Phillip?' The question was blurted out before she could stop herself, and she could tell by the fury in cold blue eyes that Stella was furious at the intrusion.

'Jealous, Heather?' she taunted.

'Not at all,' she dismissed easily. 'I was just concerned about you and Uncle Lionel.'

'I can't imagine why,' Stella snapped. 'Lionel has his work to keep him happy, and I——'

'Have Phillip,' Heather realised heavily. 'Stella——'

'For God's sake, don't start lecturing me,' the other woman rasped. 'Who am I hurting?'

The obvious answer was her husband, even if he weren't yet aware of the affair. But Heather could see that Stella was also hurting herself, that even the little softness of emotions she might once have had was buried beneath her obsession with Phillip Wingate.

'And don't claim I'm hurting Lionel,' Stella continued sarcastically. 'He hardly knows I'm alive most of the time!'

'He loves you——'

'He loves his precious airline,' the other woman snapped.

'He's giving that up to be with you——'

'Rubbish,' Stella scorned. 'The airline has always been Lionel's life.'

'Nevertheless, he's retiring early so that he can spend more time with you.' Heather frowned. 'Surely he told you that?'

'Of course he told me,' the other woman said dismissively. 'But he'll never do it.'

'But——'

'I told you, he'll never do it!' Stella insisted heatedly, her eyes feverish. 'Do you have anything to drink in this house, or is this going to be a dry dinner party?'

From the way the other woman was behaving Heather would have guessed the whisky she poured for her was far from her first drink of the evening; Stella's behaviour was positively reckless, as if she didn't care about keeping up appearances even for the sake of her marriage any more.

She tried once more to reason with her. 'About Phillip——'

'What about him?' Blue eyes were narrowed suspiciously.

'Stella, you're a married woman,' Heather reasoned impatiently. 'Uncle Lionel is sure to realise what's going on eventually——'

'I don't give a damn what Lionel finds out.' Stella slammed her glass down on the table. 'I tried to be the sort of wife he wanted, but it's killing me! I've had enough of trying to be someone I'm not!' She picked up her clutch-bag, turning to leave.

'Stella!' Heather watched her with wide eyes.

She turned, sighing. 'Don't tell me Phillip is only interested in me because I have money, because I know that already——'

'Then why——?'

'Because it doesn't matter.' She shook her

head. 'I love him anyway. He's just ambitious. Heaven knows, it's an emotion I can respect,' she added bitterly. 'And once Lionel and I are divorced, I'll be even richer from the settlement I'll demand from him, rich enough to give Phillip anything he wants.'

'Divorced . . . ?' Heather repeated numbly, having had no idea things had deteriorated this far between her uncle and his wife.

Stella nodded abruptly, every vestige of beauty drained from her face at that moment. 'I've decided to marry Phillip.'

'Even though you know he'll only be marrying you for what you can give him and not for who you are?'

Stella's mouth twisted. 'You don't seem to be too unhappy coping with the same situation!'

Heather felt all the colour drain from her cheeks at the barb. Daniel *had* married her for that reason, but it was different now, or at least it was starting to be—wasn't it?

Stella laughed softly at her suddenly pained expression. 'Don't tell me you'd forgotten why Daniel married you?' she taunted.

Heather moistened dry lips. 'My marriage to Daniel is none of your business,' she rasped at last, in control again.

'Just as my affair with Phillip is none of yours,' the other woman told her lightly. 'When Lionel arrives, tell him I've gone home to pack.'

Heather gasped. 'You can't expect me to be the one to tell him——'

'Why not?' Stella taunted. 'Someone has to do it.'

'But you——'

'I've been trying for days,' the other woman stated in a bored voice. 'It never seems to be the right time. But I've had enough of this pretence; I'm going to be with the man I really love.'

Heather was dumbfounded for only seconds after the other woman had left, and then she realised she would have to be the one to avert the catastrophe that Stella's desertion of her uncle would be to him. And if Stella couldn't be made to see the stupidity of her actions it would have to be Phillip she talked to. She had no doubt that as soon as Stella had packed she would go to Phillip's apartment, but Heather intended speaking to him first. If all Phillip were interested in were money . . .

'When Mr Taggart and my uncle arrive could you tell them I've taken my aunt home because she isn't feeling well,' she quickly told Shilton on her way out of the door. 'Please don't ask,' she groaned at his puzzled expression, knowing the other woman had left alone minutes before.

He looked affronted. 'I wasn't going to.'

No, of course he wasn't; Shilton could be relied upon to be completely discreet. 'Thank you.' She gave him a grateful smile, as she hurried out to her car.

She had no doubt her uncle would be worried about his wife, and Daniel would be equally concerned about her need to go with the other woman, but there was nothing else she could do in the circumstances. Even Stella seemed convinced her lover was a complete mercenary, it would just be a question of who could offer him the most inducement, her aunt in persuading him to marry her, or her in making him leave. She had no doubt that without Phillip in her life Stella would be quite happy to stay with her husband.

Her meeting with Phillip didn't go quite as smoothly as she had hoped it would.

'Why should I end things with Stella?' he challenged her scornfully.

'Because I've just offered you more money than she'll ever have,' Heather reminded him impatiently.

'It isn't enough,' he shrugged.

She drew in a furious breath, wondering how she could ever have found this man attractive; he now seemed totally repulsive to her. 'How much more do you want?'

'All of it,' he told her abruptly.

Her eyes widened. 'You expect me to hand all my money over to you?'

'No.'

'But——'

'I want all the money, your half of AI—and you,' he explained softly.

'You're insane!' she scorned disbelievingly.

He looked at her coldly. 'I wasted a whole

year of my life courting a woman who married someone else because he could give her more than I could,' he snapped. 'I'm not insane, Heather, I just want what's due to me. And the chance to show that arrogant bastard you married that he can't push me around,' he added harshly. 'And he'll know that as soon as you've divorced him and married me, and I've sold your share of AI to Public Airlines, the way I originally intended to do!'

Heather felt a shiver of apprehension down her spine at his vehemence towards Daniel. 'I can't do that——'

'Not because you're happy with him?' Phillip derided.

She frowned. 'Stella hasn't told you . . . ?'

His mouth twisted. 'We never talk about you—for some reason the mere mention of your name throws Stella into a rage!'

Heather sighed, shaking her head. 'Then you don't know that if I divorce Daniel I lose everything? That if I hadn't married him when I did my half of Air International would have been sold off and the money distributed to charity?'

Phillip's expression darkened dangerously. 'You're lying——'

'It's the truth, Phillip.' She didn't add that she had wanted to marry Daniel any way that she could. 'My father's will was explicit.'

He looked at her searchingly, sinking down into a chair as he saw the truth in her eyes. 'But why?' His voice was strangulated.

She sighed. 'Because that was the way my father wanted it, and even in death he wouldn't be thwarted. Will you take the money I offered, Phillip, and leave Stella alone?' she prompted softly.

He looked up at her as if he had never seen her before. 'Leave Stella alone?' he repeated harshly. 'Why the hell should I?'

'Because——'

'—you offered me money,' he finished coldly. 'Stella and I are two of a kind, Heather,' he told her. 'We know each other's faults and we accept them.'

Her eyes widened. 'You love her . . . '

'Did you think I was incapable of loving anyone?' he rasped.

'No. But——'

'I can be myself with Stella, we get on well together. I'll take your money, Heather, but I'll take Stella, too,' he told her challengingly.

'What on earth makes you think that I——'

'Does your husband know of your little visit to me tonight?' he mocked, smiling his satisfaction as she paled. 'Things might be all right between the two of you, Heather, but not good enough for him to believe this was just a platonic visit to an old friend!'

She had been a fool to think she could ever reason with this man. And Stella knew exactly what he was like. Maybe the two of them deserved each other after all! She couldn't believe her uncle wouldn't be better off without a woman who thought so little of him that she could fall in love with a man like Phillip Wingate.

'I won't be blackmailed——'

'Won't you?' taunted Phillip. 'Oh, I think you will.'

Heather turned and left the apartment, her footsteps hurrying as his mocking laughter followed her.

CHAPTER ELEVEN

IT BEGAN to snow on the drive back to the house, the fierce wind whipping it into a severe storm, and it took all Heather's concentration to stay on the road, that intensity not allowing time for thoughts of how she could tell her uncle his wife had left him. How *could* she tell him something like that?

As she finally turned the car into the driveway up to the house she groaned her dismay at seeing her uncle's car already parked there, knowing the two men must have arrived in her absence. She didn't even have time to collect her thoughts together before facing her uncle.

She was momentarily diverted from the unwelcome task when she saw that Daniel wasn't with her uncle; she had presumed his car was in the garage.

'He had to fly up to Manchester unexpectedly,' her uncle explained regretfully. 'We have some personnel problems there.'

She could have done with Daniel's moral support at this moment, not knowing how to break the news to her uncle about Stella; and the weather was hardly suitable for Daniel to be flying anywhere, she thought worriedly.

'I was just about to leave myself to see how Stella is now,' her uncle continued lightly. 'Shilton told me about your having to take her home.'

'Er—Uncle Lionel——'

'Was it another migraine?' He frowned his concern. 'She's had several of them lately. Maybe I should insist she see a doctor——'

'Uncle Lionel, Stella has left you!' Heather stared at him with wide eyes once she had made the outburst, no longer able to continue listening to his concern about a woman who wasn't worthy of it, groaning her own distress as he paled and seemed to stagger. 'Uncle Lionel, she—there was someone else,' she explained quickly as she helped him to sit down. 'She isn't worthy of this,' she choked as he buried his face in his hands and began to sob.

His head snapped back at that. 'What do you know about it?' he demanded fiercely. 'She's my wife, damn it. My *wife!* Of course she's worth it!'

It broke her heart to see the man who had always loved and cared for her reduced to this aching shadow of himself.

'I have to go to her.' He rose unsteadily to his feet. 'I'm sure we can talk this out.'

'I'm afraid it may be too late for that——'

'No!' he rasped, shaking his head disbelievingly. 'I love Stella. She's my life!'

'She's gone, Uncle Lionel.' Heather clutched his arm. 'She left here to pack. I followed her, but—it was no good.' She didn't intend telling him of her visit to Phillip Wingate. 'She's gone, Uncle,' she said again heavily.

He became suddenly still. 'Gone where?'

She gnawed at her bottom lip. 'I don't know where,' she said evasively, not wanting him to go to Phillip's apartment in this mood.

His eyes narrowed, and he suddenly looked much older than his years. 'You said there was someone else . . . ?'

Why had she told him that? It was bad enough that Stella had left him at all, without this further humiliation. 'Yes,' she confirmed reluctantly.

'You mean she was having an affair?' he rasped.

Heather couldn't remember a time when Stella *wasn't* having an affair—with someone. 'You had no idea?' she frowned.

'Of course I had no idea,' her uncle snapped harshly. 'Otherwise I would have done something to stop it! I knew she'd been unhappy lately, discontented, but I thought it was something that would pass with time, and I intended retiring next month so that I could be with her more . . . '

'I'm sure Daniel would be only too happy to have you stay on if you want to reconsider that decision——'

'Now that I no longer have a wife to spend more time *with*,' he finished abruptly.

'Uncle Lionel——'

'I have to see Stella,' he told her raggedly.

'Talk some sense into her——'

'She was leaving as soon as she'd finished packing,' Heather interrupted gently. 'Why don't you telephone the house——?'

'I have to *see* her——'

'The weather is foul tonight.' The howling wind and snow was getting worse. She hoped Daniel hadn't been silly enough to insist on flying to Manchester in this weather, no matter what the problem. 'Telephone the house and see if Stella is still there first,' she encouraged, sighing her relief when he picked up the the receiver to dial his home number.

She took the opportunity to tell Shilton that none of them would be requiring dinner after all, giving her uncle this moment of privacy, hating Stella for doing this to him in this public way, giving him no chance to hide his pain and heartbreak.

He was sitting in the armchair when she came back into the room, and one look at the defeated droop of his shoulders and the agonised expression on his face told her that Stella had definitely gone.

'You're sleeping here tonight, Uncle Lionel,' she told him briskly. 'Your room is ready for you, and——'

'She didn't even say goodbye,' he said wonderingly, not seeming to have heard Heather at all. 'After five years together she didn't even leave me a letter. Mrs Lloyd said she just took her things and left.'

Heather swallowed hard. Stella was a selfish bitch, a——

'There must be something I can do to bring her back,' her uncle muttered. 'Some way I can persuade her to——'

'Uncle Lionel, please,' she choked her distress at seeing him so broken. 'I know this is painful for you——'

'How could you know?' he scorned harshly. 'You and Daniel didn't marry for love!'

'That may be true, but I've always loved Daniel,' she told him steadily, knowing he was just hitting out in his pain, turning as a soft knock sounded on the door before it was quietly opened. 'Yes, Shilton?' She was grateful for his interruption, wanting to give her uncle time to regain his control.

The manservant looked uncomfortable, realising he had interrupted at a very private moment. 'Mr Taggart is on the telephone, madam. He said I wasn't to disturb you if you were eating dinner, but in the circumstances . . . ?'

Daniel! 'I'll take the call, thank you, Shilton,' she said with some relief.

'I'll go up to the room you've had prepared for me,' her uncle said quickly, squeezing her arm as he went past. 'I'm sorry,' he told her gruffly.

Heather watched with pained eyes as he wearily left the room before turning to pick up the receiver. 'Daniel!' she cried joyfully.

'What's wrong?' The frown could be heard in his voice.

'I'm just so glad you rang.' She sank down into a chair.

'The weather isn't quite as bad up here——'

'You're already in Manchester?' She groaned her dismay, having hoped to stop him before he left.

'Yes.' He sounded puzzled now. 'Heather, has something happened? Shilton said that the dinner party has been cancelled, that Stella had to leave early.'

'She's left Uncle Lionel,' she choked. 'Just packed up and left him. I've invited him to stay here for the night, but he seems convinced he can persuade Stella to come back to him, and I'm just as sure he can't. And——'

'Calm down, darling,' Daniel soothed. 'And start from the beginning.'

That 'darling' was enough to soothe her jagged nerves, and she told him everything that had happened during the evening, omitting nothing—not even her visit to Phillip. She wouldn't be blackmailed by a man like him, and Daniel had to start trusting her some time; now was as good a time as any. She held her breath as she waited to find out if her uncle would be consoling *her* before the night was through.

'I'll deal with Wingate another time,' grated Daniel. 'Are you OK?'

Relief flooded through her. 'Fine. I'm

worried about Uncle Lionel, though; he's taken this very badly.'

'I'd "take it very badly", too, if you left me,' he said harshly.

Her breath caught in her throat. 'You would?'

'I think we need to talk when I get back home, Heather,' he bit out.

'When will that be?' She still sounded breathless.

'I'm on my way now,' he told her briskly. 'A couple of hours at most.'

'Daniel, I love you.' She hadn't told him that since last night in his arms, and somehow she needed to tell him now. 'I love you!'

'I—we'll talk when I get back,' he repeated harshly. 'Go and get some rest now; I guarantee you won't be sleeping once I get home,' he added throatily.

Heather rang off to stand at the window, staring out at the storm-tossed night. What a strange evening it had been, a traumatic one for her uncle, and yet Daniel's words had held a promise for the two of them. Could he have come to love her, after all? God, she hoped so, she knew she couldn't bear to go through the pain her uncle was suffering because of his love for Stella.

She left Shilton to lock up for the night, knowing Daniel would prefer to let himself in when he arrived home, then checked on her uncle, pleased to see he was asleep, although he lay fully clothed on top of the bed. Sleep was the best thing for him, she decided, as she went to her own room. He would be able to think more clearly in the morning.

She had been dozing for some time when she heard the telephone ring in the hallway, just about to transfer the call up to the bedroom when the ringing stopped and she heard a voice downstairs. She had thought her uncle was still asleep, hadn't heard him go downstairs earlier. As she pulled on her robe she heard him make another call out, and he was just replacing the receiver as she reached the bottom of the stairs.

'What is it?' she gasped at his stricken look, his face very grey. 'Stella?' she prompted.

He shook his head woodenly, his mouth opening but no words coming out.

'Uncle Lionel!' She was becoming really panicky now. 'Tell me!'

'The first call was a reporter, trying to locate Daniel. I—it——'

'What's happened?' Her nails dug into his flesh as she clutched his arm.

'He—he wanted to know who'd been travelling on the small private AI jet tonight,' he related haltingly. 'I—it—he said——I rang the airport, managed to speak to someone there who believed I was who I said I was. It seems—they said the plane crashed at the end of the runway, that it—blew up,' he added faintly. 'There are no survivors, everyone on board was killed instantly. Heather, Daniel was on that plane!' He cried what she had already guessed he was trying to tell her.

Her *whole life* had been on that plane, was all wrapped up in Daniel; she *refused* to believe that he was dead!

She shook her head. 'There's been a mistake——'

'Heather——'

'I tell you there's been a mistake!' she insisted vehemently at his reasoning tone. 'Daniel can't be—he's still alive!' Her voice broke emotionally. 'I would *know* if he—if he were dead!'

'They say the plane exploded, Heather.'

'Then Daniel wasn't on it——'

'We both know he *was* on it,' her uncle put in softly.

'No.' She shook her head, swallowing down the tears that threatened. 'I refuse——It can't be true!' she bit out forcefully, turning towards the stairs. 'I'm going to get dressed and go over there.'

'The police will be here soon.' Her uncle stopped her. 'They'll know by now that Daniel was the one on board——'

'No!' she cried, collapsing down on to the bottom stair, shaking uncontrollably as the tears cascaded down her cheeks. 'It can't be true! It can't be true!' She repeated the words over and over again, her arms clasped about her knees as she swayed backwards and forwards in her grief. 'I only spoke to him a short time ago, told him how much I loved him. He was coming back to me, Uncle Lionel, he was going to tell me how much he loved me; I *know* he was,' she added fiercely.

'Darling, don't.' Her uncle sat down beside her, taking her in his arms to hold her tightly against his chest.

'Don't call me that,' she choked.

'What . . . ?' He gently caressed her hair.

'Darling,' she sobbed. 'It's what Daniel——Oh, God, I have to go to the airport!' She pulled out of his arms. 'They could be wrong, Daniel might still be alive.' Her eyes were feverish. 'He could have been blown clear. Maybe——'

'Heather, don't do this to yourself,' her uncle groaned. 'He's gone, Daniel's gone.'

The same words she had used to tell him Stella had left him, and yet they weren't the same at all; Daniel had *really* gone, and she would never see him again.

A numbed calm settled over her, her breathing ragged. 'I still have to go to the airport,' she told her uncle flatly. 'The police can talk to me there if they have to,' she added as he seemed about to argue. 'I *am* going, Uncle Lionel.'

'I wish you wouldn't,' he sighed. 'It isn't going to be very pleasant. But if you insist,' he calmed her heated protest, 'then I'll drive you.'

She was grateful for the offer, she wasn't sure she would have been able to drive herself if she had tried, and she went to her room to dress, her movements automatic, moving as if in a daze.

But, as she dressed, the numbness began to pass, and in its place was a raw ache that cried out with pain every time she tried to imagine life without Daniel. Until they showed her—until they proved——She couldn't accept that she would never see him again, never be able to tell him she loved him, never be able to hold him in her arms again.

A heart-wrenching sob dragged at her throat, and her knees gave way beneath her.

Her uncle found her collapsed on the carpeted floor, where Daniel had once made love to her, sobbing out her grief and pain.

She looked up at him. 'Why Daniel?' she cried. 'Why him?'

'Why the hell not?' Something seemed to snap inside him. 'Do you think the two of you have some God-given right to be happy?'

Heather rose slowly to her feet, stepping away from him, sure that her grief had to be giving her hallucinations; her uncle couldn't have said that! 'You don't really mean that . . .'

'We all die some time,' he scorned. 'Why shouldn't it be Daniel's turn now?'

Stella's leaving him had to have unbalanced him, she couldn't think of any other reason he would be acting in this way; he had *liked* Daniel.

'Why should you have Daniel when Stella has left me?' he demanded fiercely. 'It's because of the two of you that Stella left at all!'

'Daniel and I?' she gasped. 'But——'

'AI should have been mine,' he told her savagely. 'I worked as Max's assistant all those years, helped him build it up into the success it is today.' In his fevered anger he overlooked the fact that a couple of years ago, before Daniel stepped in to help, it had been a faltering airline! 'And instead of coming to me as it should have done, it now belongs to a man Max despised, and a woman who wasn't even his real daughter! Stella would never have thought of leaving me if AI had come to me as it should have done!'

That he was probably speaking the truth wasn't to Stella's credit at all, but that didn't seem to worry him, his love for her was all-consuming. Even to making him glad that a man was dead, the man Heather loved!

She swallowed hard. 'I'm going to the airport now. Daniel may not be dead——'

'He is,' her uncle rasped. 'Can't you understand that there were no survivors, that——'

'Stop it.' She put her hands over her ears. 'Stop it! I don't want to listen to any more!'

'Then don't listen,' her uncle jeered. 'Go to the airport. But he's gone, Heather, just as Stella has gone from me.'

She shook her head, turning to run down the stairs, grabbing up her keys from the hall table before running outside.

The wind and snow was an icy blast against her body as she unlocked her car, grateful that she had pulled on a sweater and denims earlier, just wanting to escape from the house now, not wanting to delay while she got a coat.

She couldn't believe her uncle had said those things, that he was *glad* Daniel was dead! Tears streamed down her cheeks, her hands tightly gripping the steering-wheel as she fought for control. The car slid precariously on the snow-covered driveway and, as she slowly approached the end of it, bright head-lights blinded her. Heather felt the control slip completely from her grasp as she swerved to avoid those blazing lights.

The car slid sideways, going off the driveway on to the grass before coming to a grinding halt as it smashed into the huge mound of snow, grass and earth that edged the driveway.

Heather was jerked forward, and then sharply back on impact, too shaken to release the catch of her seat-belt, not caring if she got out of the car or just sat there and froze to death. Why should she want to live when Daniel was dead, *dead?*

She had completely forgotten the approaching car that had caused her to panic, but she knew the other driver had come to her aid as the door beside her was wrenched open, the icy coldness it allowed in not touching her as she sat back with her eyes closed.

'Heather!' gasped a gentle voice of rough velvet. 'My God, Heather, are you all right?'

She was dreaming. Or perhaps she was already dead? Yes, maybe that was the answer. It was the only way it could be Daniel talking to her, because he was dead, too. He——

'Heather, answer me!' Painful fingers clasped her shoulders and turned her towards the cold and the sound of Daniel's voice. 'Damn it, open your eyes and answer me!' He shook her roughly.

She shouldn't be able to feel pain if she were dead. But she did feel the pain, Daniel's fingers bruising through her sweater. And she could feel the cold of the snow and wind too, now.

'Heather!' He shook her again.

Yes, it definitely hurt when he shook her like that. And if she could feel pain——!

Her lids flew open, and she looked straight into Daniel's anxiously concerned face.

CHAPTER TWELVE

'I WAS on my way home when I heard on the radio that a plane had crashed and exploded at the airport,' Daniel explained grimly. 'I didn't find out until the next news-flash that it had been an AI plane. Once I heard that, I knew you must have thought the worst, that you'd probably assumed I was on the plane.' He shook his head.

Daniel had driven the two of them back to the house some time ago, and even while they spoke to the police who arrived minutes after them, answered their questions, Heather hadn't been able to stop touching Daniel, the miracle of his being alive after all still not quite real to her.

He gave a heavy sigh. 'They must have told Jack to take off again as soon as he'd refuelled.'

'Uncle Lionel and I assumed—and no one told us any differently—that the plane had crashed on landing not take-off.' Heather shuddered. 'I still can't believe it was Stella and Phillip who were killed and not you. What do you suppose they were doing?'

'Knowing them as I do, and from what you've told me of their mood tonight, I would say it greatly appealed to their sense of humour to use an AI plane to go on a victory trip,' he rasped. 'As a member of the family, Stella was at liberty to order Jack to take her anywhere she chose to go.'

'Poor Jack. And poor Uncle Lionel,' she groaned. 'He loved Stella so much.'

'Too much,' Daniel bit out. 'It wasn't a healthy love.'

'She can't hurt him any more,' Heather choked.

Her uncle had refused to believe the police when they told him his wife was dead; he had rushed out of the house to drive to the airport to see for himself, much as she had done when she thought it had been Daniel on the plane. Her uncle hadn't made it as far as his car, the strain of the last few hours was too much for him as he fell to the ground clutching his chest, the heart attack sudden—and final.

Heather gave a shaky sigh. 'I never thought how hurt he must have been to have been omitted from Max's will in that way,' she groaned. 'That fifty-one per cent of Air International should really have gone to him; he worked most of his life for it.'

'You were Max's daughter, it was obvious——'

'But I wasn't!' She stood up agitatedly, her hands twisting together as she avoided Daniel's puzzled gaze. 'Which must only have made what happened worse for my uncle.' She straightened. 'You once asked what I'd done to Max for him to have worded his will the way he did.' She drew in a ragged breath. 'At the time, I told you I hadn't been the son he wanted. There was more to it than that.' She finally met his gaze. 'I wasn't his *daughter*, either.' She shook her head. 'My mother was already pregnant with me by another man when she married him.'

Daniel looked stunned. 'Did he know that?'

'Oh, yes.' She gave a shaky smile. 'It was the reason he married her. You see, he was incapable of fathering a child himself,' she revealed breathlessly.

His face darkened angrily. 'He knew that?'

Heather frowned at his reaction. 'Oh yes, he always knew that.'

Daniel stood up to pace the room forcefully. 'The bastard!' he finally exclaimed. 'My God, I'm glad that *neither one* of us is related to a man like that!'

She became suddenly still. 'What do you mean?'

His mouth twisted. 'Did you never wonder why I agreed to help Max with his faltering airline . . . ?'

She frowned. 'I thought you considered it to be a good business deal.'

'Or why I put up with his sadistic habit of humiliating me?' Daniel rasped.

She had always wondered why a man as strong and honest as Daniel had stood Max's treatment of him . . .

'Why I daren't let myself so much as touch you because I knew that if I did I wouldn't be able to stop?' he continued harshly. 'Even though I always wanted you, too!'

She swallowed hard. 'Daniel . . . ?'

His eyes glowed fiercely silver. 'For two years, until just before he died, when he took pleasure in telling me the truth, I believed that Max was *my* father, that you were my *sister*!'

Heather sat down heavily. 'How——? I don't understand . . . ' she said weakly, completely dazed by the revelation. Sister? How could——?

Daniel looked furious. 'When my mother died I found some letters, old letters that she had kept for years, proving that she'd had an affair with Max Danvers about the time I was conceived. I went to see him, and was instantly struck by the similarity in our colouring. I confronted him with his affair with my mother, asked him if he could be my father, and he—the bastard greeted me like the long-lost son he'd never known existed! And I *believed* him!'

'Oh, Daniel!' Heather cried in her anguish for the pain he had suffered.

He nodded abruptly. 'It was only after the deal for my financial participation in AI had been finalised that he began to show how he really felt towards me. Even then I thought maybe it was because he was frightened I'd try to get him to acknowledge his illegitimate son into his nicely respectable world. Just before he died he told me the truth, that my mother had been involved with several men when he knew her, that whoever my father was it certainly wasn't him.'

Poor Daniel. He had been searching most of his life for the man who had fathered him, only to have the reality turn into a nightmare. 'What he did to you was so cruel——'

'No crueller than what he did to you,' Daniel rasped harshly. 'Shilton knew about it, didn't he?'

'I wasn't the son Max wanted,' she shrugged. 'The son he married my mother to acquire.'

'And I came along claiming to *be* the son he knew he could never have,' Daniel realised bitterly. 'My God, how he must have laughed at that.'

And the bitterness could so easily ruin Daniel's life a second time, make him forget what they had together. 'But he didn't win, Daniel, can't you see that?' Heather encouraged eagerly. 'He forced the two of us to marry, knew that you would be contemptuous of me just because you believed I *was* his child, was sure that we would never actually find happiness together. But we have,' she said with certainty. 'Daniel, we have!'

He looked at her searchingly. 'Why did you marry me, Heather?'

She gave a serene smile. 'For the only reason I would ever marry anyone, because I love you.'

He drew in a sharp breath. 'Did Max know how you felt about me?'

She moistened her lips. 'I didn't think

so . . . but yes, I'm sure he did. Daniel, can't you see I *had* to marry you, even knowing how mercenary it made me look? I wanted the airline to be yours! And *I* wanted to be your woman!'

Daniel closed his eyes as if in severe pain. 'Do you have any idea what it was like to be attracted to you and feel that it was wrong, so very wrong?' he groaned.

'Max liked to hurt people,' she sighed painfully.

He shook his head. 'I fought against caring for you for so long that even when it became possible for me to marry you I didn't want to love you. You're right, I resented you because you were his daughter, because I believed you had to be like him. On our wedding night——'

'Don't,' she groaned, still feeling the shame of that night. 'I acted very badly——'

'You *acted* that way because it was the role I'd forced you into,' he corrected grimly. 'The signs of your innocence were all there for me to see, I just chose to ignore them, preferred to think the worst because it was easier that way. Easier for me.'

'You'd been hurt——'

'That's no excuse for the way I've treated you,' he cut in self-disgustedly. 'Heather, I have something for you, something I—I've been carrying around for days but been afraid to give you.'

Afraid? Daniel was never afraid! 'What——?'

'Don't look like that,' he groaned at her
stricken look, enfolding her in his arms. 'It's
something I should have given you months
ago, something I should have *told* you months
ago.' He reached into his jacket pocket. 'With
my love.' He handed her a velvet box.

Heather's hands trembled as she stared at
him with wide eyes. His *love*, he had said. Did
he mean it?

'Aren't you going to open it?' he chided
gruffly, looking uncertain.

She couldn't bear to see him any less than
arrogantly self-confident, awkwardly flicking
open the lid to the box she held, her eyes
glowing as brightly as the sapphire and
diamond ring she had uncovered.

'If you don't like it we can change it.' Daniel
hastened into speech at her silence. 'I—it's an
engagement ring. I thought——'

'You love me!' She threw her arms joyously
about his neck. 'You really love me!'

His arms closed about her possessively.
'Until the day I die!'

CHAPTER THIRTEEN

HEATHER had been watching for the approach of the car, running lightly to the door as she saw the headlights through the raging blizzard. She had been so worried . . .

The droplet earrings that swung against her neck were a perfect match for the ring that nestled against her wedding band on her left hand.

She threw open the door in anticipation, unconcerned by the snow being blown into the house as she launched herself into the arms of her laughing husband. 'I thought you were going to be delayed by the weather,' she told him between kisses.

'Nothing could keep me from coming home to you,' Daniel assured her gruffly.

'I hope you're feeling strong,' she grinned. 'We're all ready to decorate the Christmas tree.'

'*We* are?' he murmured indulgently, his arm about her shoulders as they walked through to the lounge.

'We are,' she nodded, bending down to scoop up the tiny bundle of mischief from the play-pen. 'We've been waiting for *hours*, haven't we, darling?' She nuzzled against her son's throat, making him chuckle.

The advancement of her pregnancy, already five months along by the time Daniel insisted she see a doctor about her tiredness and weight increase, had come as a complete surprise to them both, her body having played a trick on her and not given her the usual sign that would have told her she was expecting Daniel's child. At seven months old, Master Jason Taggart was the most treasured thing in their marriage, apart from their deep love for each other.

The baby smiled at his father, proudly displaying the four teeth that had been recent acquisitions, holding out his arms to the man he adored.

Heather watched the two of them together, their relationship unmistakable, both being dark-haired and grey-eyed. It was only the second Christmas she and Daniel had shared, their first as a family, and it was a time they had all been looking forward to.

A shadow darkened her eyes.

'What is it?' Daniel was instantly attuned to her mood, interesting Jason in the buttons on his jacket as he frowned his concern at Heather.

'Uncle Lionel,' she explained sadly. 'I wish things could have been different for him.'

'Darling,' Daniel squeezed her hand sympathetically, 'he wouldn't have wanted to live without Stella, the heart attack was kinder.'

'You're right.' She shook off her sadness for what might have been, smiling brightly. 'Now let's get this tree decorated; Father Christmas has all those presents to wrap up yet!'

'My present doesn't need any wrapping,' Daniel murmured throatily.

They shared a smile of complete intimacy. '*That* present isn't going to be under the tree tonight,' Heather said huskily.

Daniel looked at the tree, and then at the glowing fireplace. 'No, I don't think it will be!' He put Jason down, the baby instantly crawling to the box of brightly coloured decorations he had been denied touching all day. 'That rug looks much more comfortable,' Daniel told Heather softly as he took her in his arms. 'I love you, Mrs Taggart.'

'And I adore you, Mr Taggart,' she answered with feeling.

A family. They had become their own family, needing no one else but each other and Jason, and the other children they hoped to have. They were a *real* family.

Harlequin Presents

Coming Next Month

Available in March wherever paperback books are sold, or through Harlequin Reader Service:

In the U.S.
901 Fuhrmann Blvd.
P.O. Box 1397
Buffalo, N.Y. 14240-1397

In Canada
P.O. Box 603
Fort Erie, Ontario
L2A 5X3

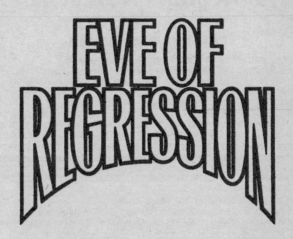

Take 4 books
& a surprise gift
FREE

SPECIAL LIMITED-TIME OFFER

Mail to   Harlequin Reader Service®

In the U.S.   In Canada
901 Fuhrmann Blvd.   P.O. Box 609
P.O. Box 1394   Fort Erie, Ontario
Buffalo, N.Y. 14240-1394   L2A 5X3

YES!   Please send me 4 free Harlequin Romance® novels
and my free surprise gift. Then send me 8 brand-new novels every
month as they come off the presses. Bill me at the low price of
$1.99 each*—an 11% saving off the retail price. There are no
shipping, handling or other hidden costs. There is no minimum
number of books I must purchase. I can always return a shipment
and cancel at any time. Even if I never buy another book from
Harlequin, the 4 free novels and the surprise gift are mine to keep
forever.   118 BPR BP7F

*Plus 89¢ postage and handling per shipment in Canada.

Name   (PLEASE PRINT)

Address   Apt. No.

City   State/Prov.   Zip/Postal Code

This offer is limited to one order per household and not valid to present
subscribers. Price is subject to change.   DOR-SUB-1D

America's most beloved romance novelist, author of the bestselling ENCHANTED,

PATRICIA MATTHEWS

returns with her newest spellbinding historical romance:

Thursday and the Lady

Patricia Matthews explores America's most unforgettable era and once again creates a novel of passion as only she can!
